ING

BUNBUN
&BONBON

FANCY FRIENDS

graphix

An Imprint of

SCHOLASTIC

To Sayuri & Dav, Ken & Jonah —
the fanciest (and loveliest!) of friends.

Library of Congress Control Number: 2019957360

ISBN 978-1-338-64683-2 (hardcover)
ISBN 978-1-338-64682-5 (paperback)

10 9 8 7 6 5 4 3 2 1   20 21 22 23 24

Printed in China   62
First edition, September 2020
Edited by Ken Geist and Jonah Newman
Book design by Phil Falco and Steve Ponzo
Color assistance: Wes Dzioba
Creative Director: Phil Falco
Publisher: David Saylor

CONTENTS

5

WHEN BUNBUN MET BONBON

25

TEAM FANCY!

35

A FANCY GARDEN PARTY!

49

DONUTS FOR LUNCH!

57

**BEST FRIENDS FOREVER
AND EVER!**

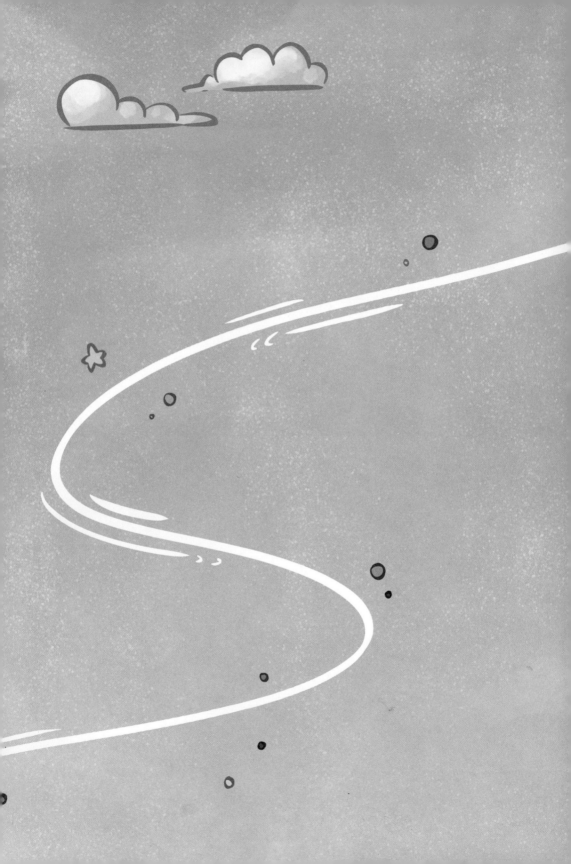

WHEN BUNBUN
MET BONBON

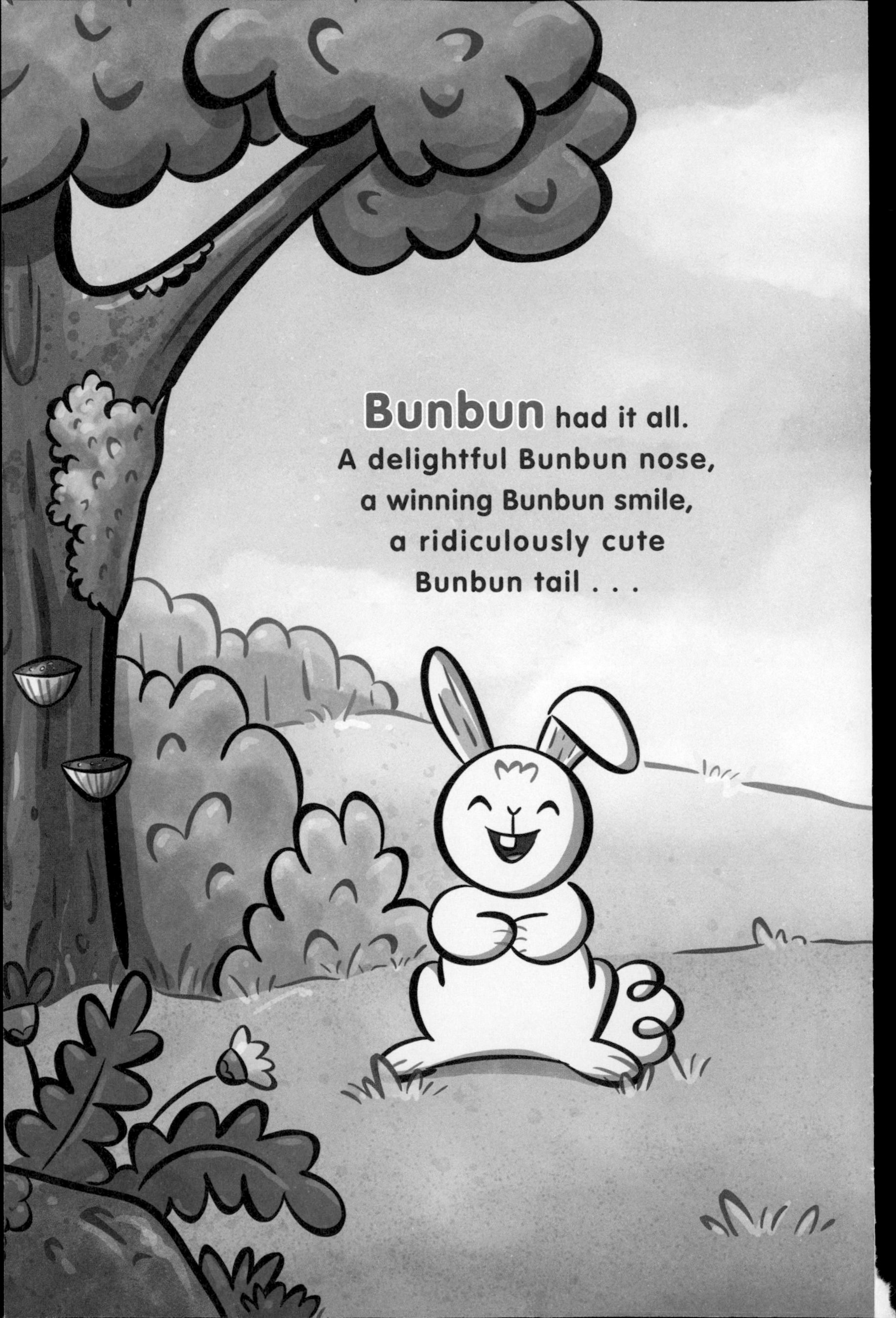

Bunbun had it all.
A delightful Bunbun nose,
a winning Bunbun smile,
a ridiculously cute
Bunbun tail . . .

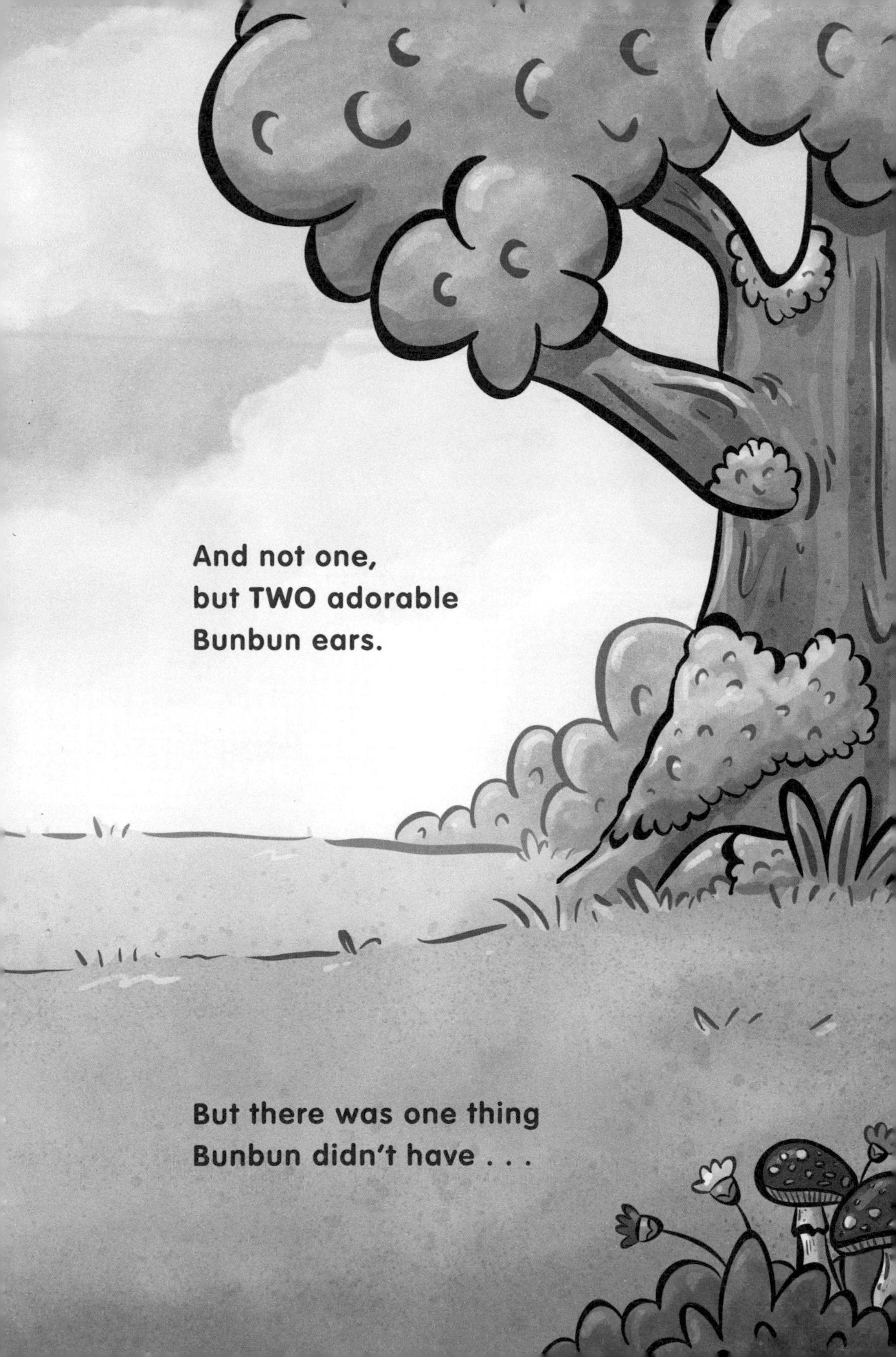

And not one,
but TWO adorable
Bunbun ears.

But there was one thing
Bunbun didn't have . . .

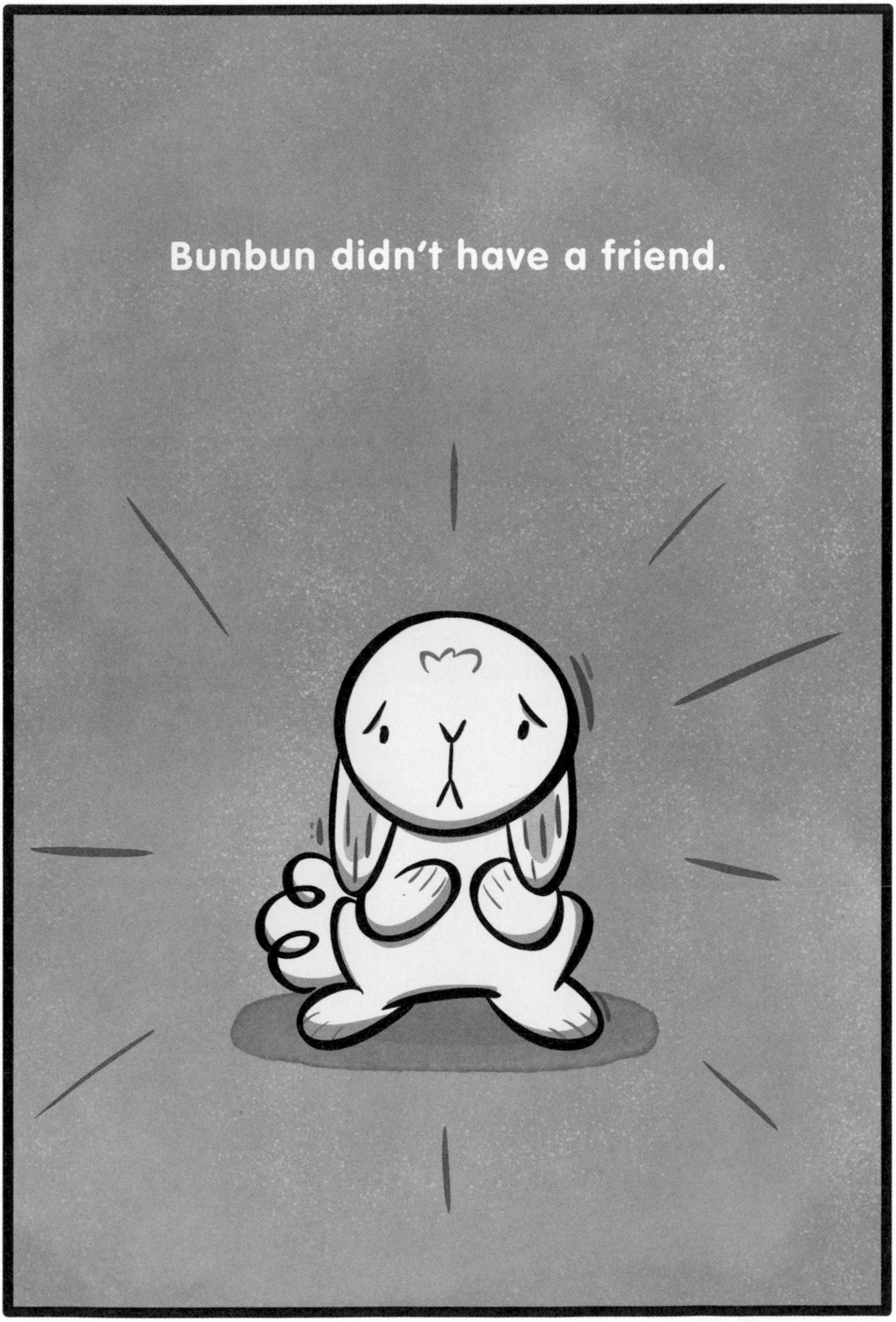
Bunbun didn't have a friend.

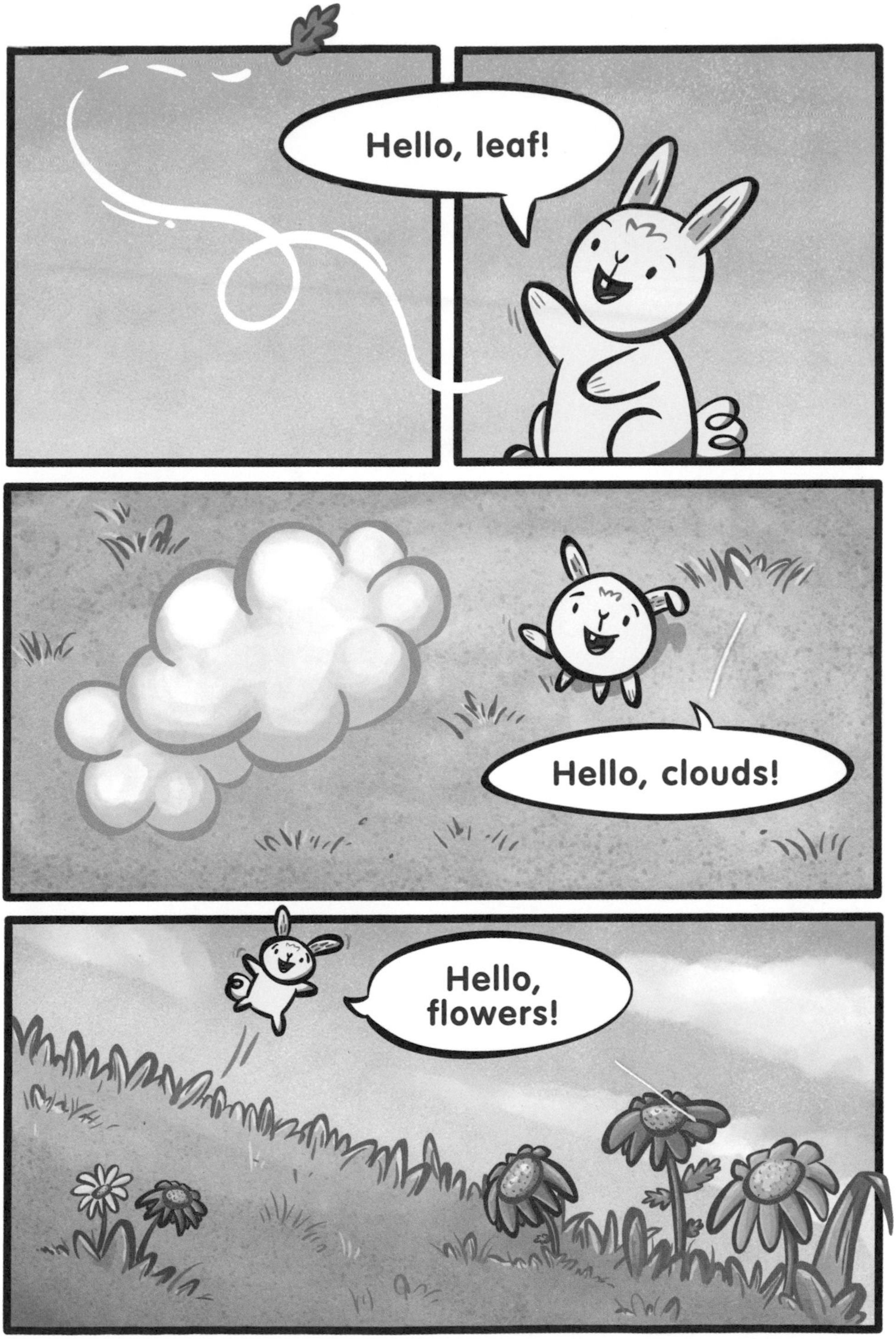
Hello, leaf!
Hello, clouds!
Hello, flowers!

Hello, pond!
Hello, stick!
Hello, bird!

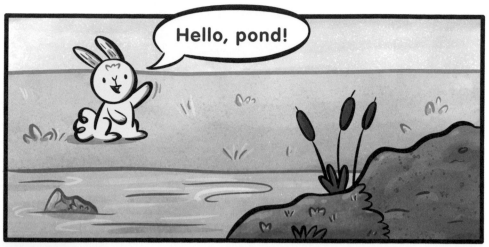

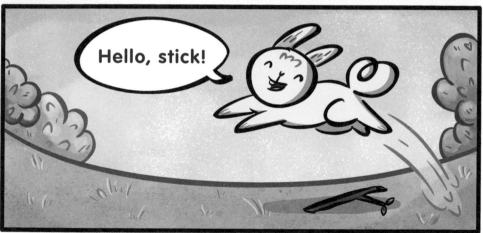

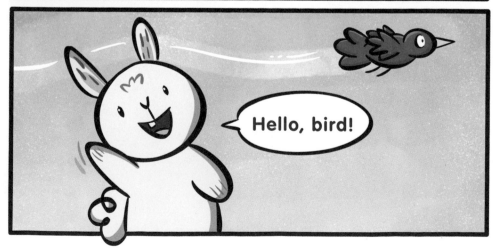

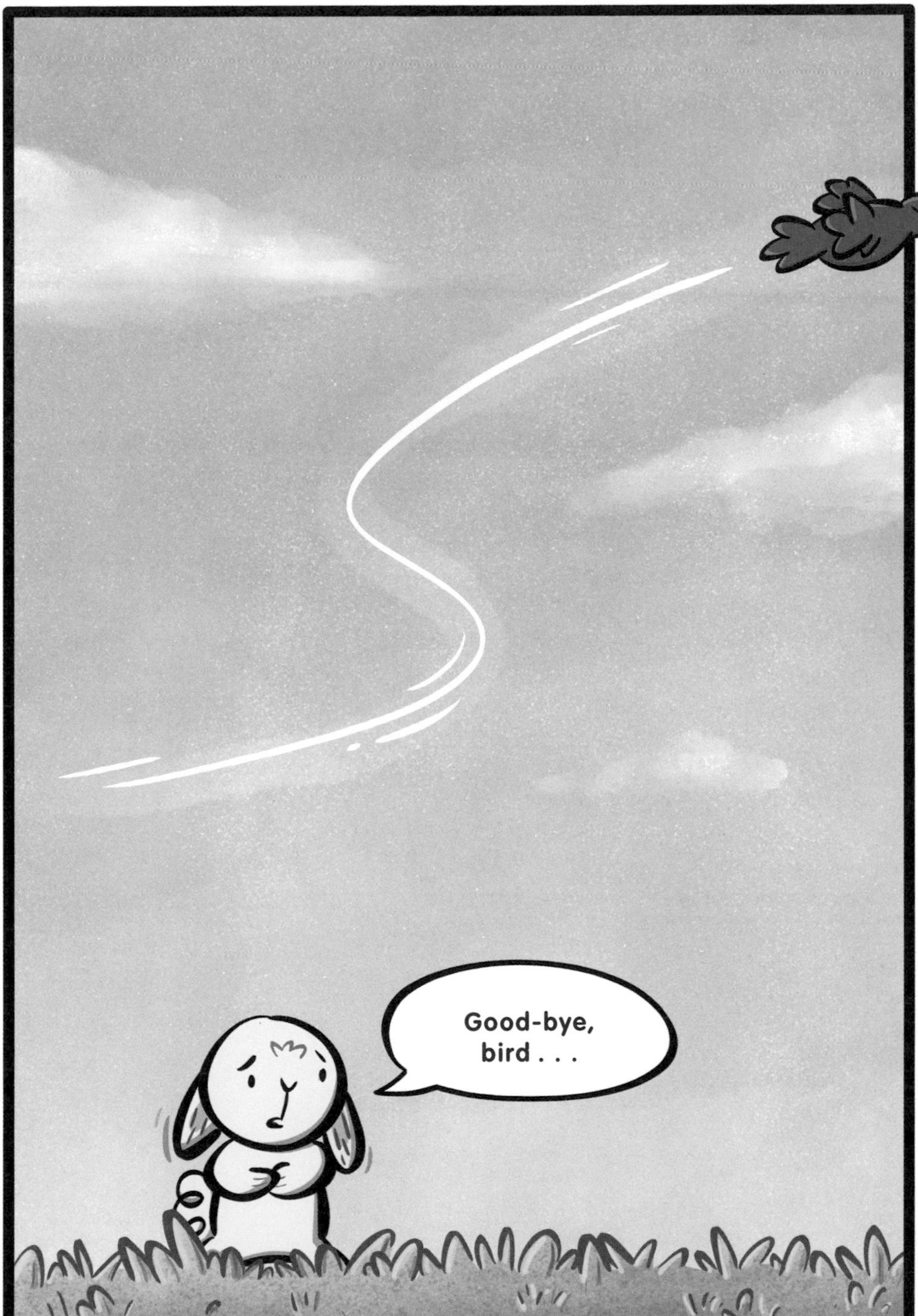
Good-bye,
bird . . .

UNTIL ONE DAY . . .

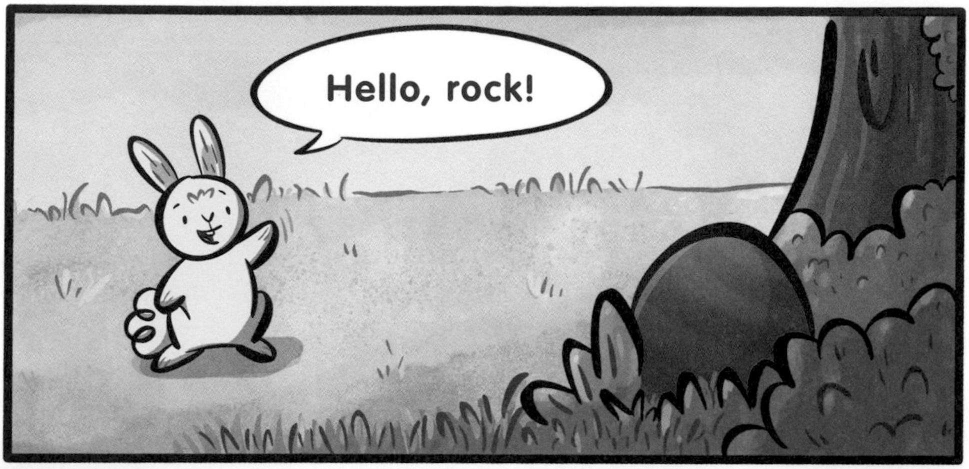
Hello, rock!

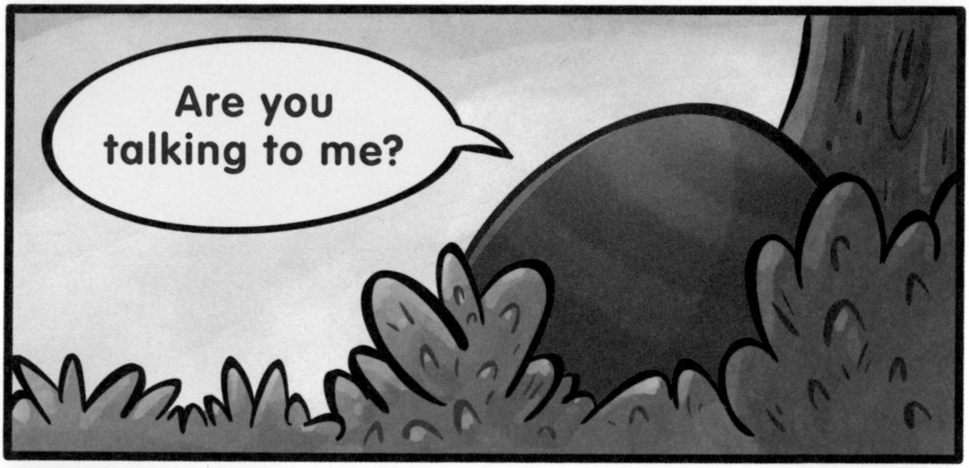
Are you talking to me?

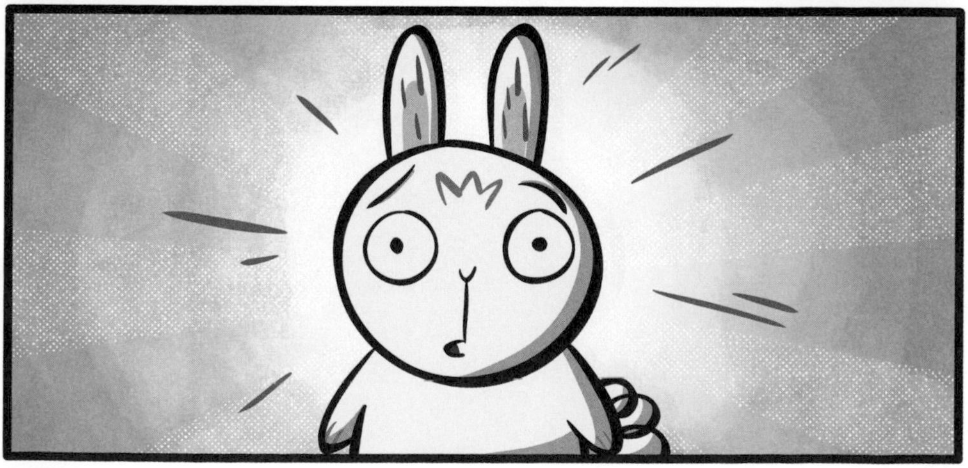

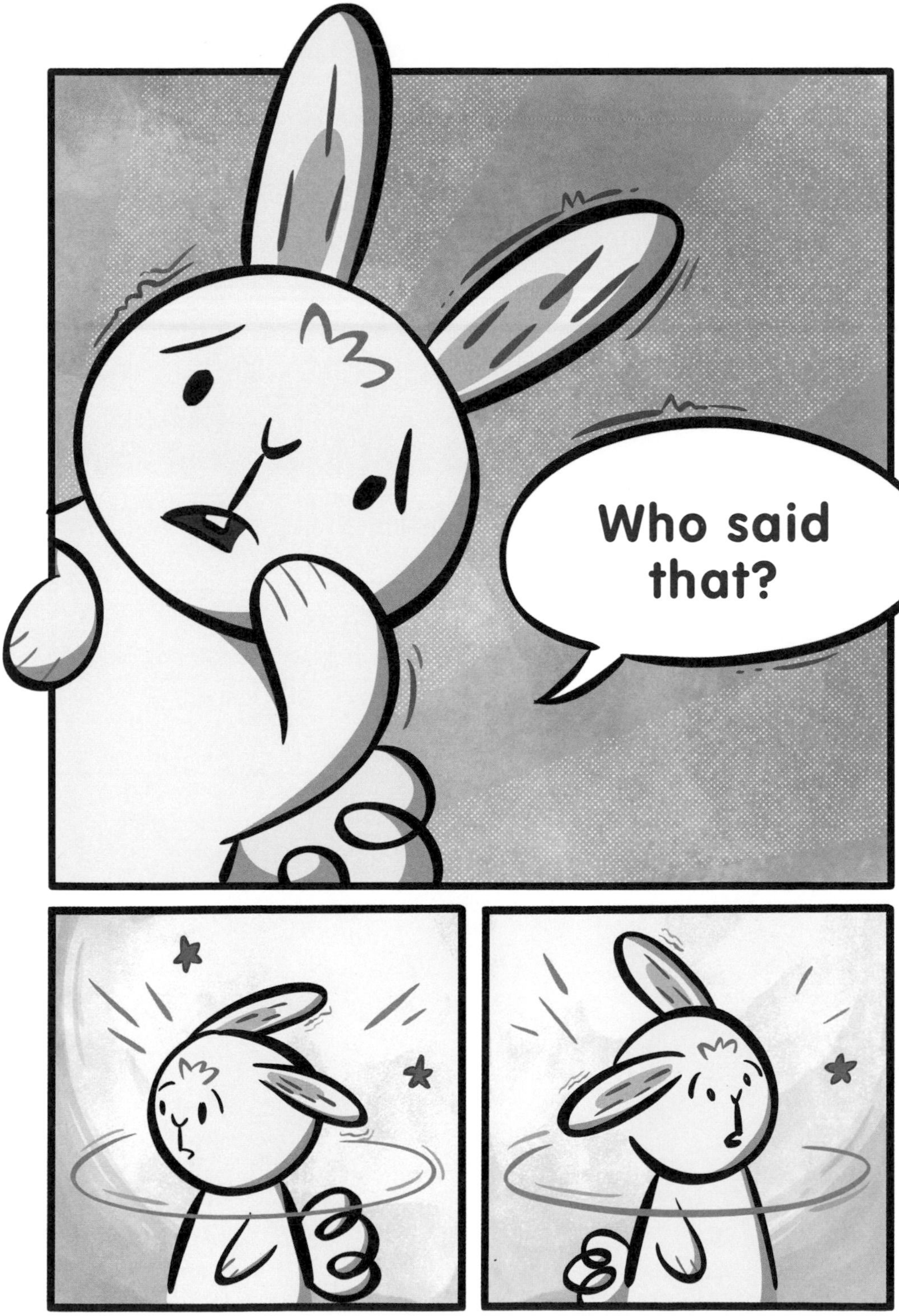
Who said that?

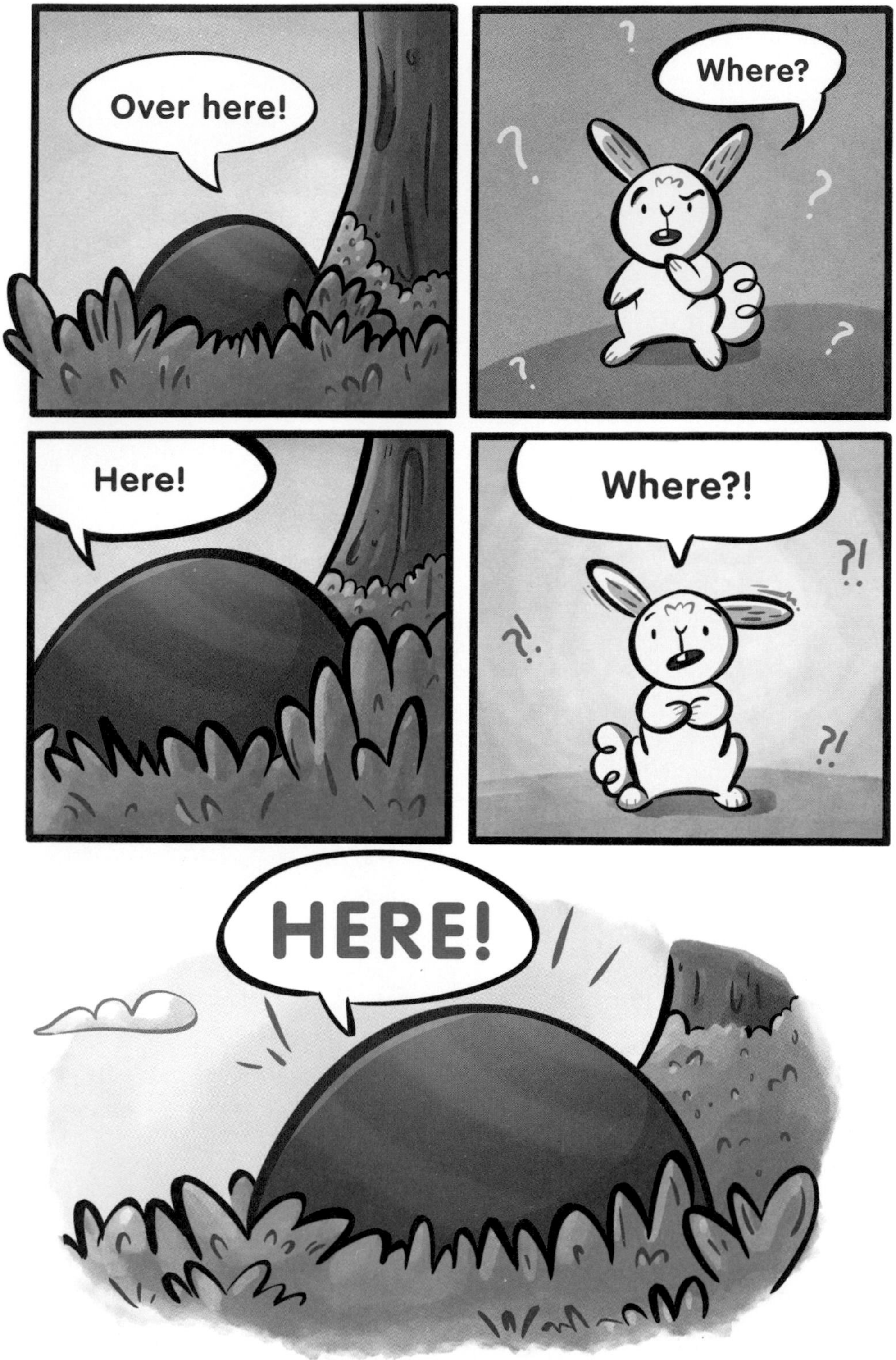
Over here!
Where?
? ? ? ? ?
Here!
Where?!
?! ?! ?!
HERE!

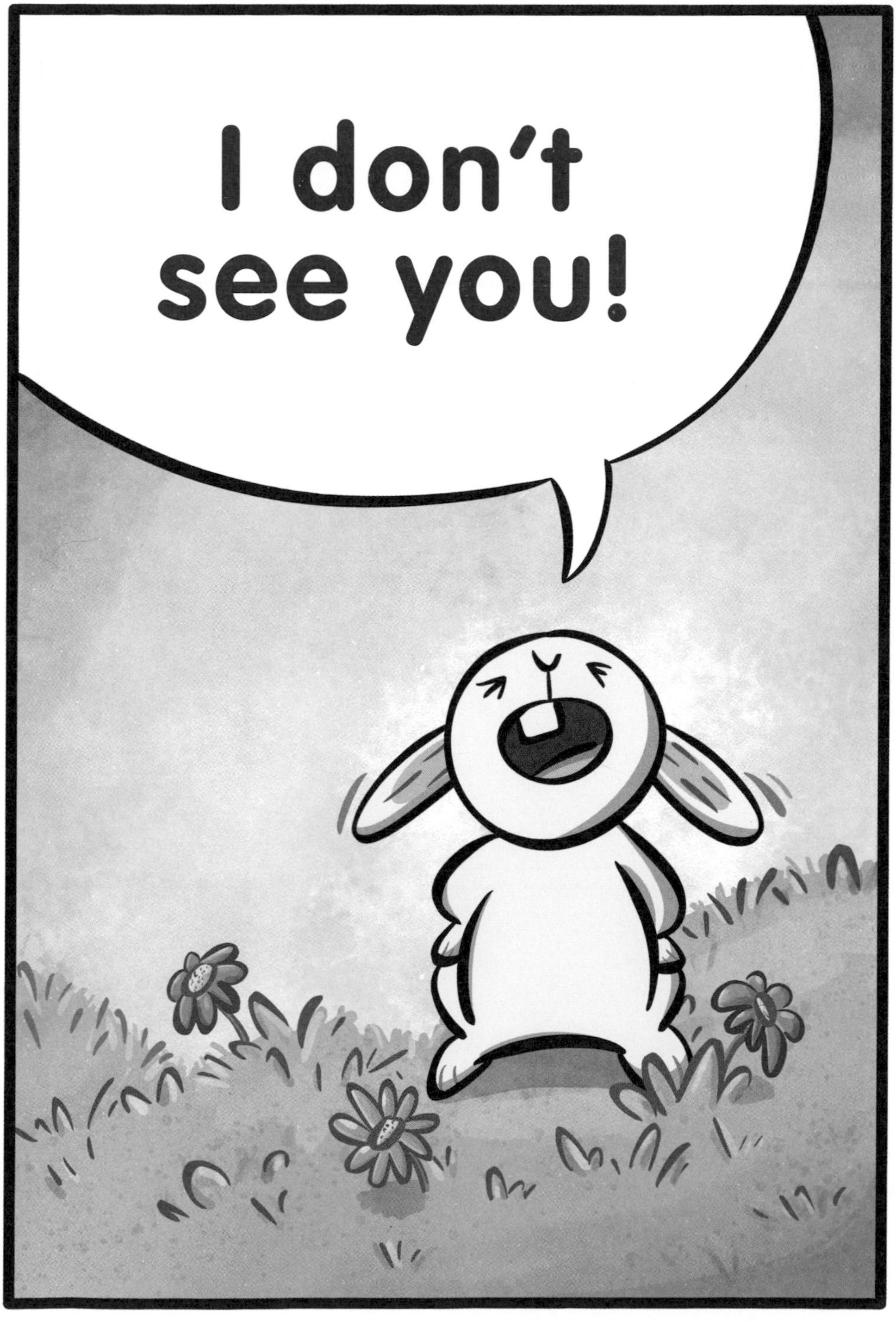
I don't see you!

bwoing

Hi!

Whoa, a talking rock!

I am not.

You are so! I can hear you with my spectacular ears.

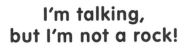

I'm talking, but I'm not a rock!

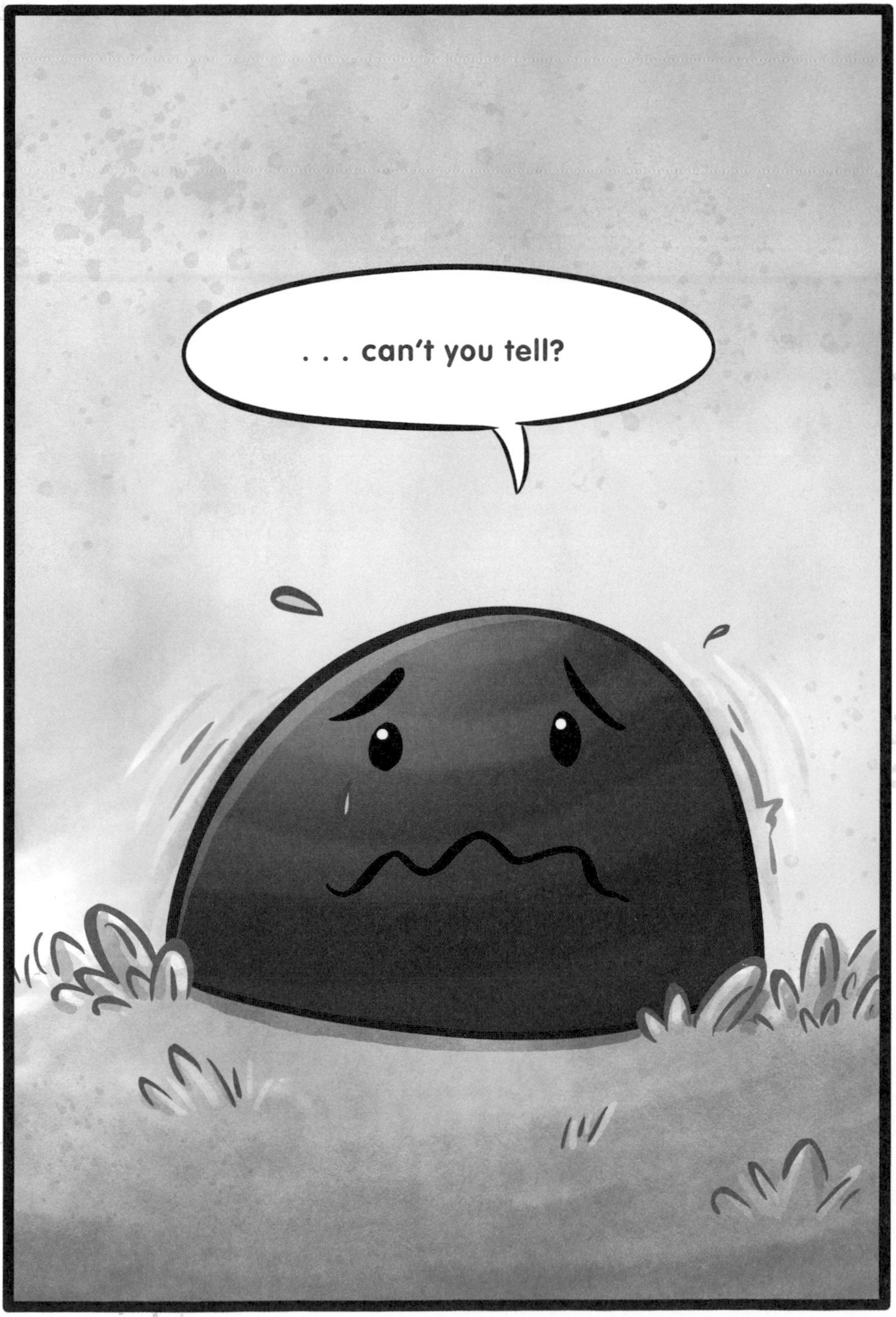
. . . can't you tell?

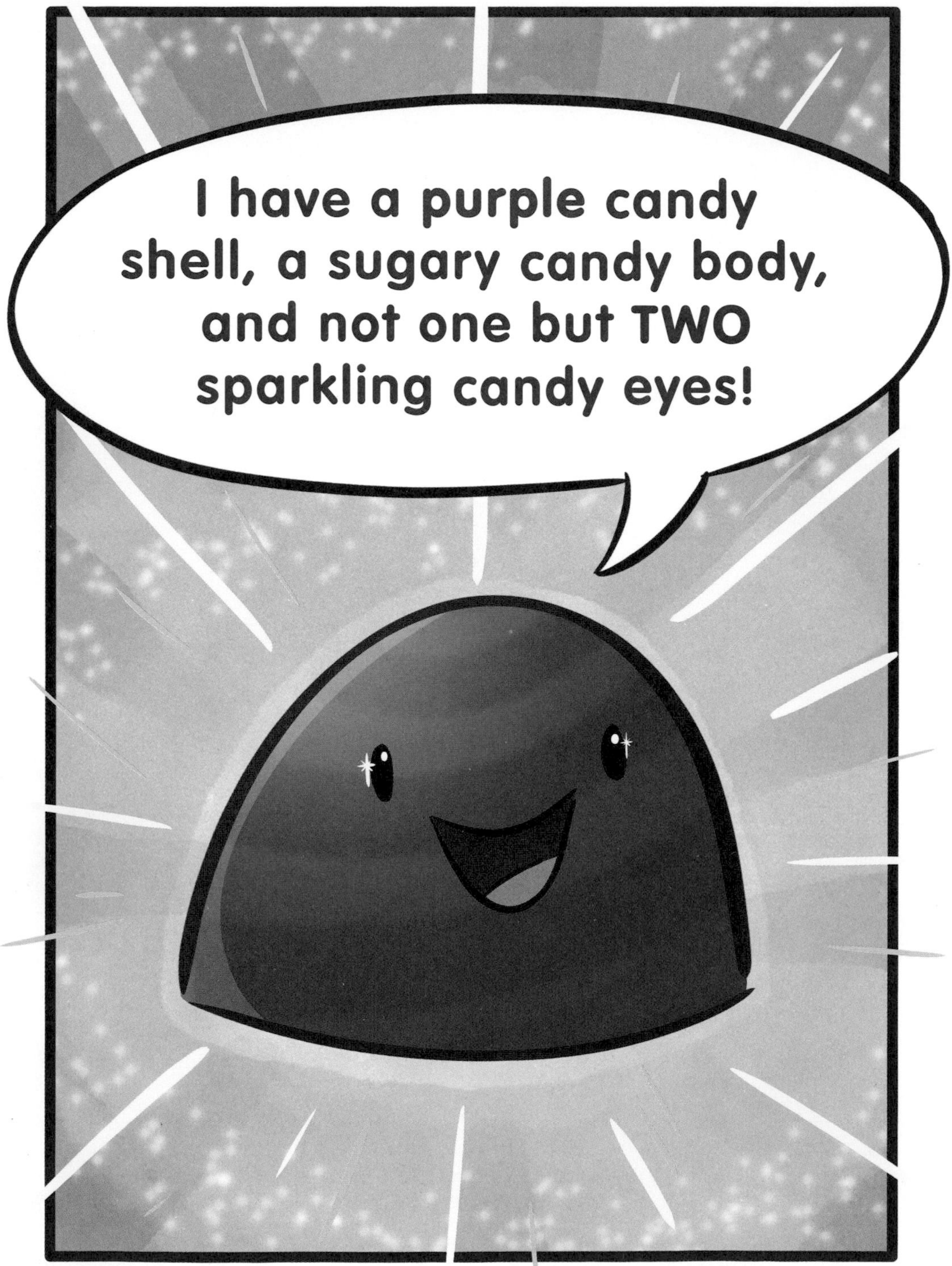
I have a purple candy shell, a sugary candy body, and not one but TWO sparkling candy eyes!

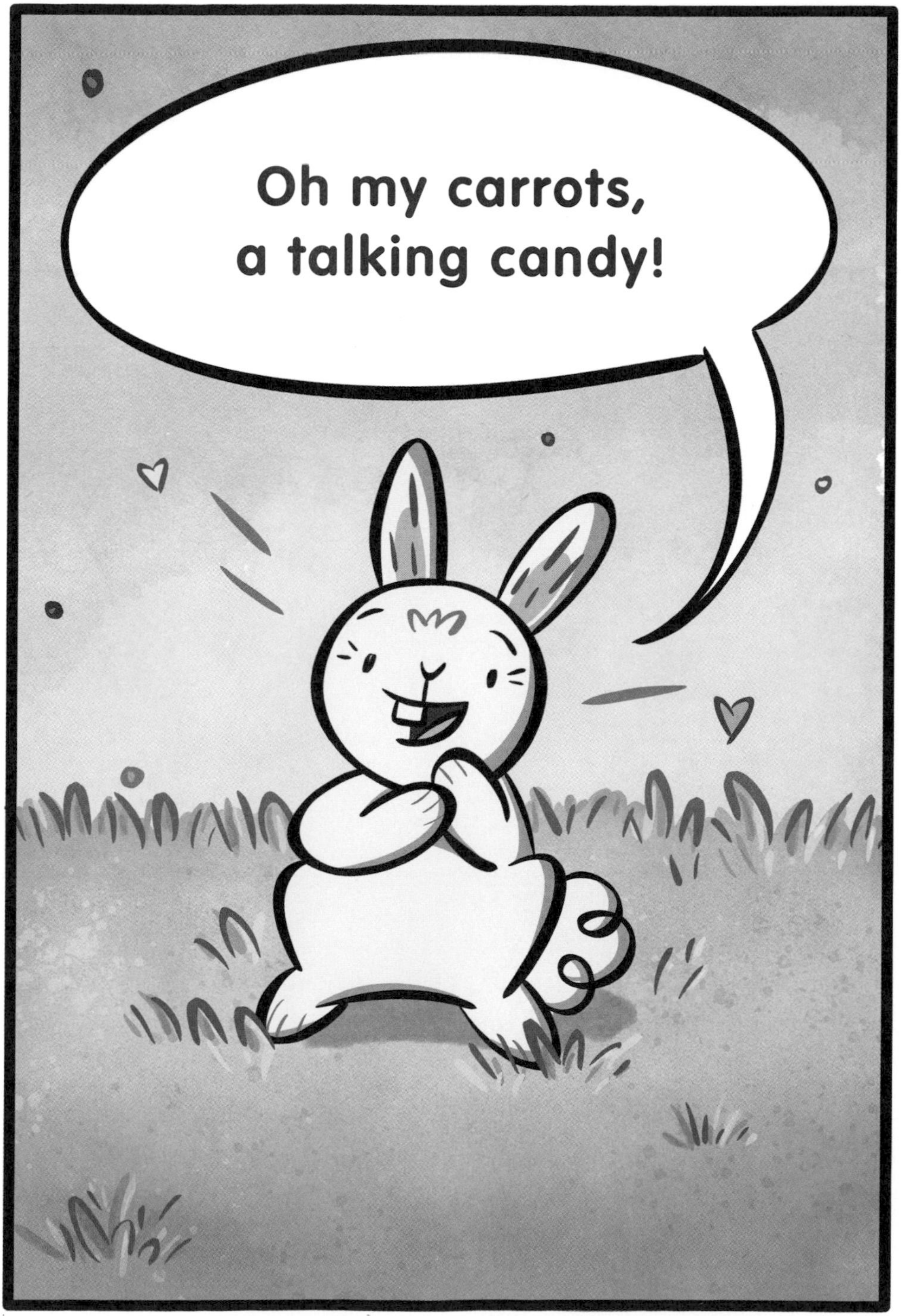
Oh my carrots,
a talking candy!

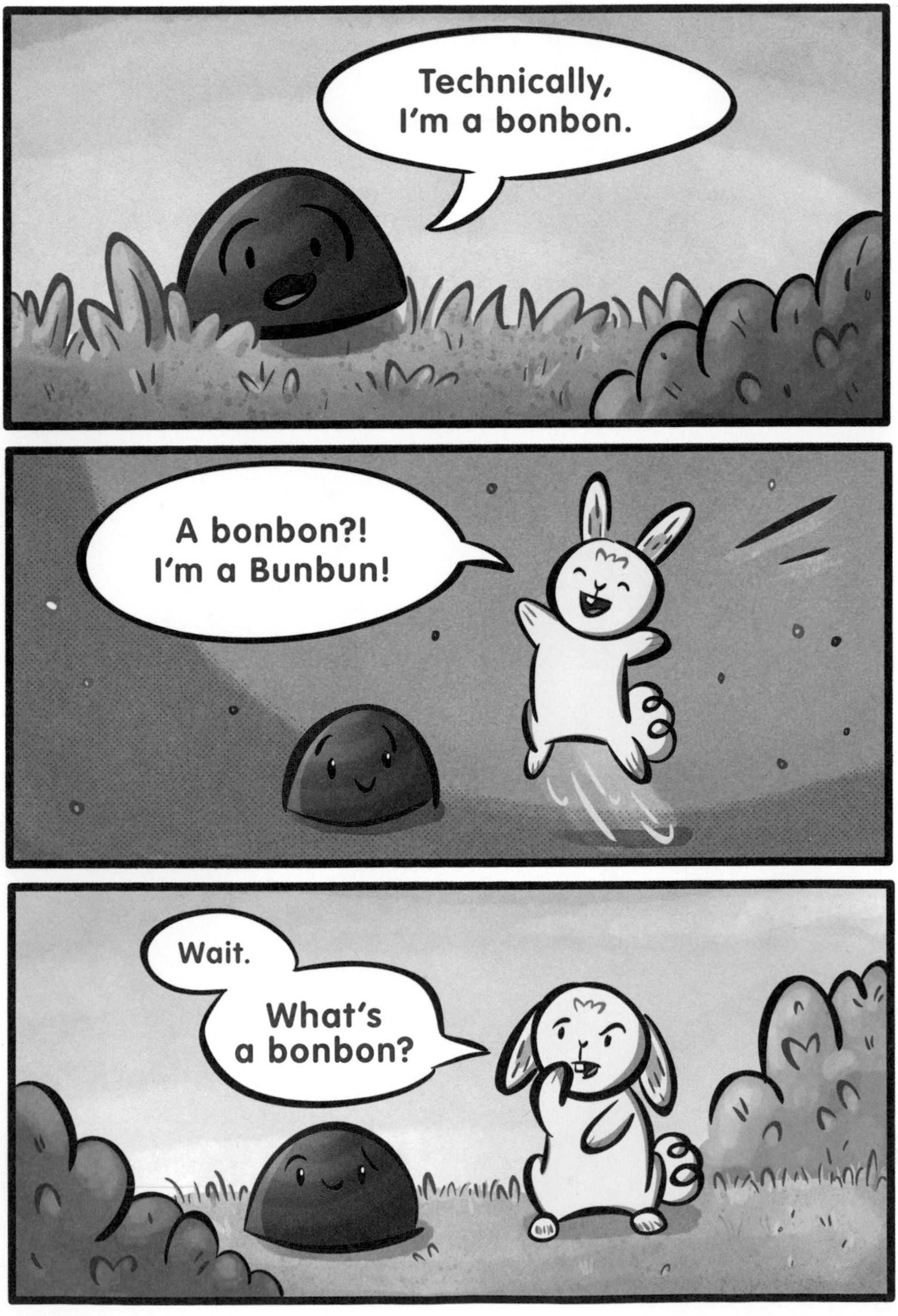
Technically,
I'm a bonbon.
A bonbon?!
I'm a Bunbun!
Wait.
What's
a bonbon?

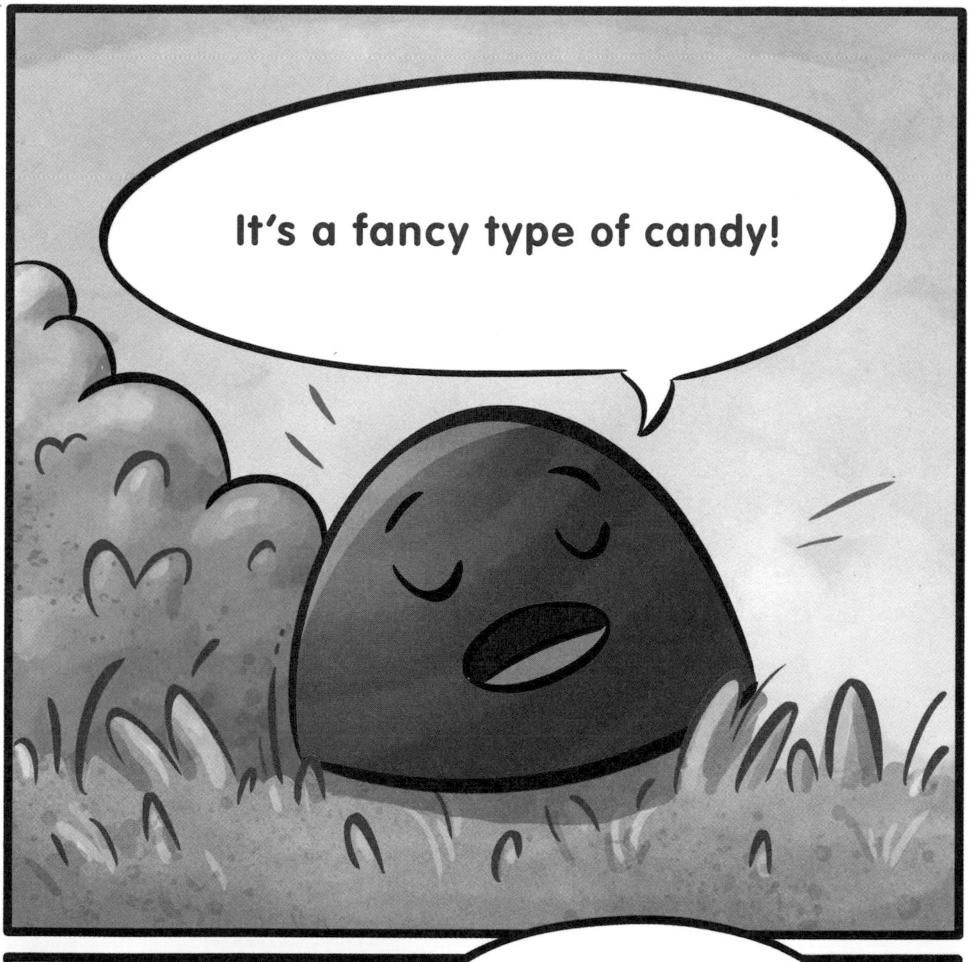
It's a fancy type of candy!

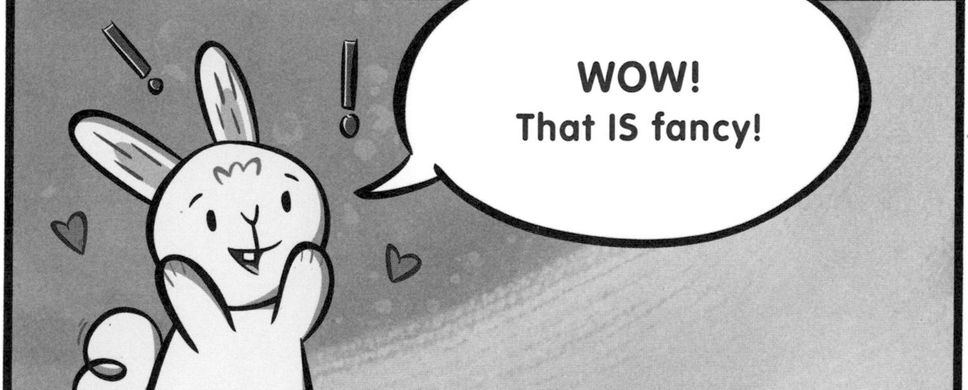
WOW!
That IS fancy!

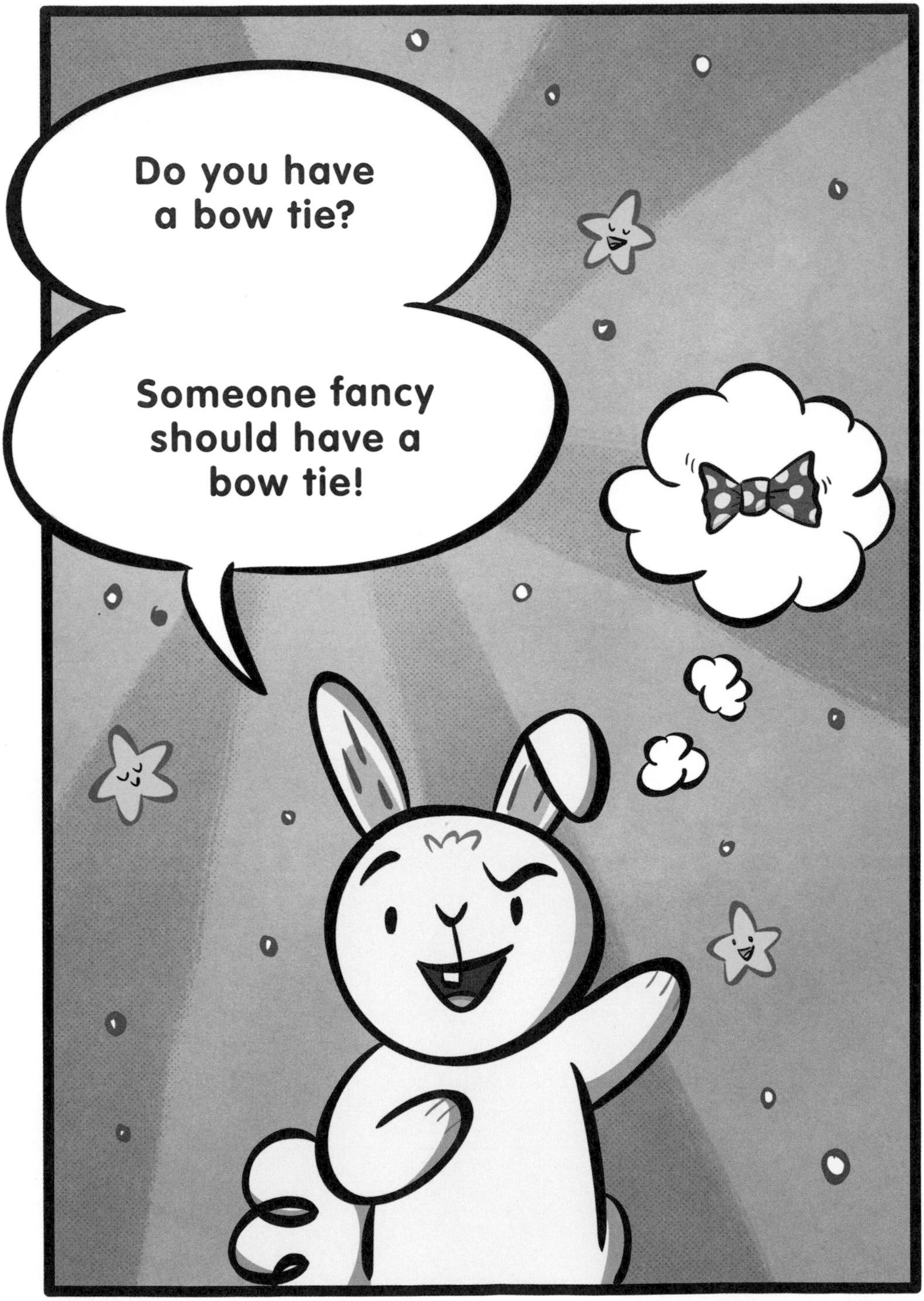
Do you have a bow tie?
Someone fancy should have a bow tie!

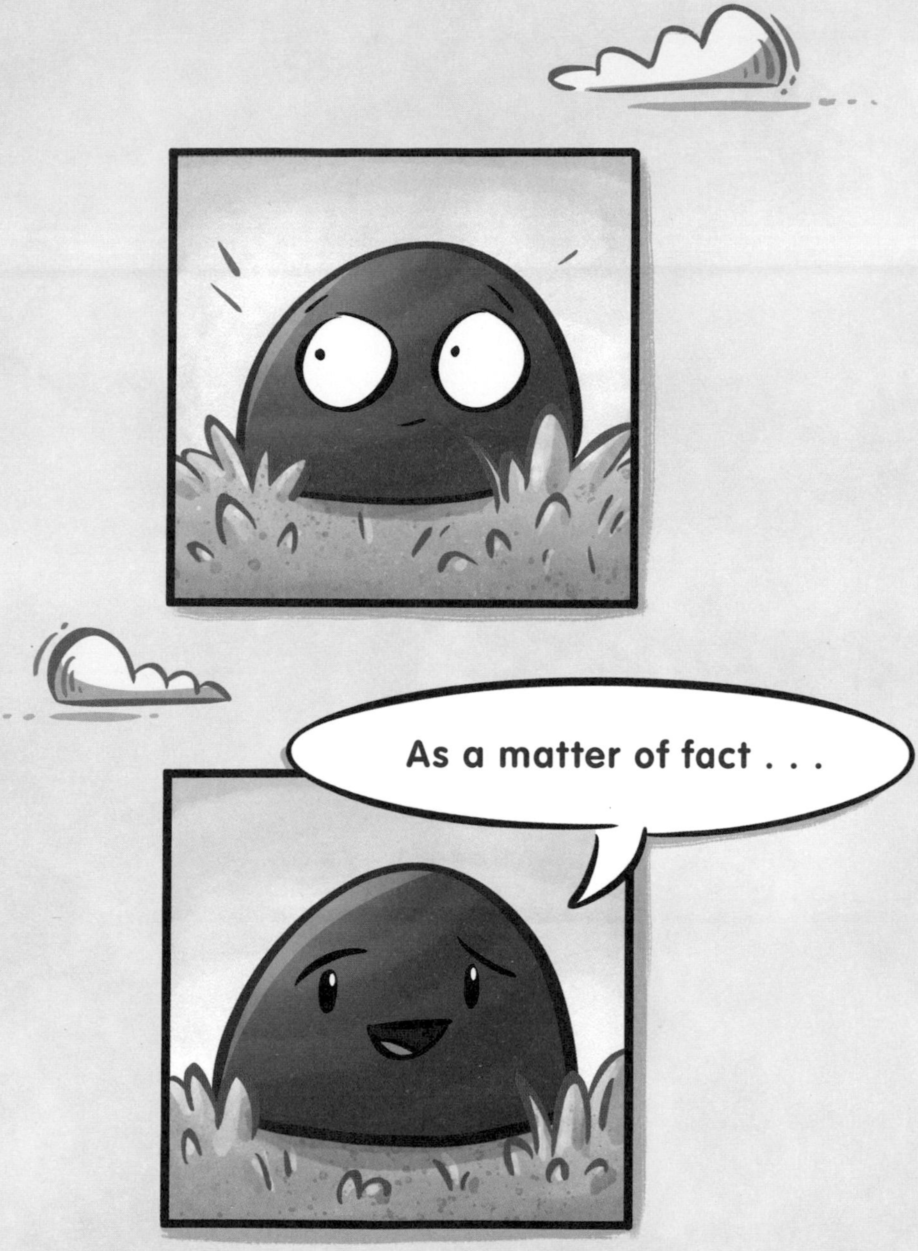
As a matter of fact . . .

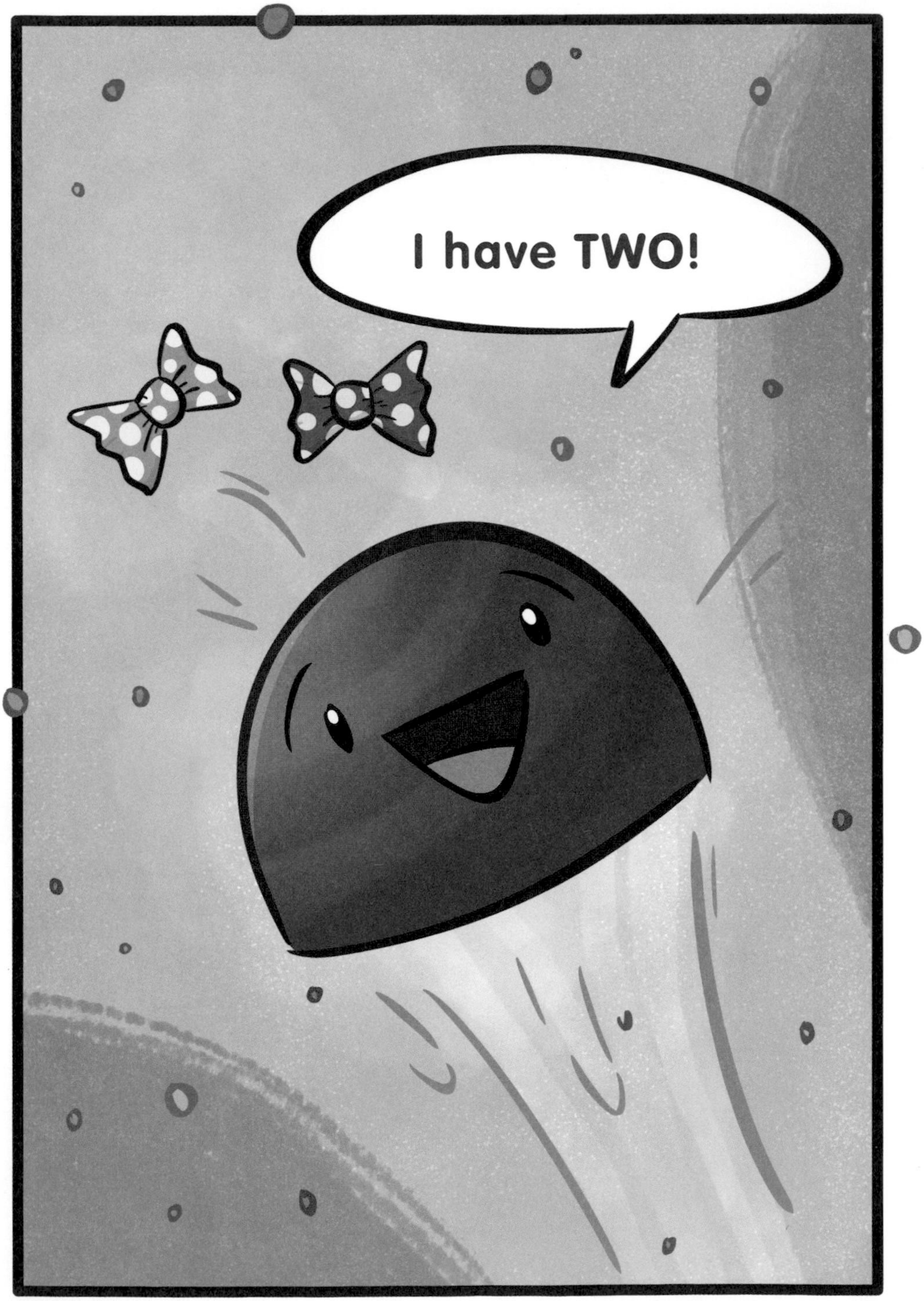
I have TWO!

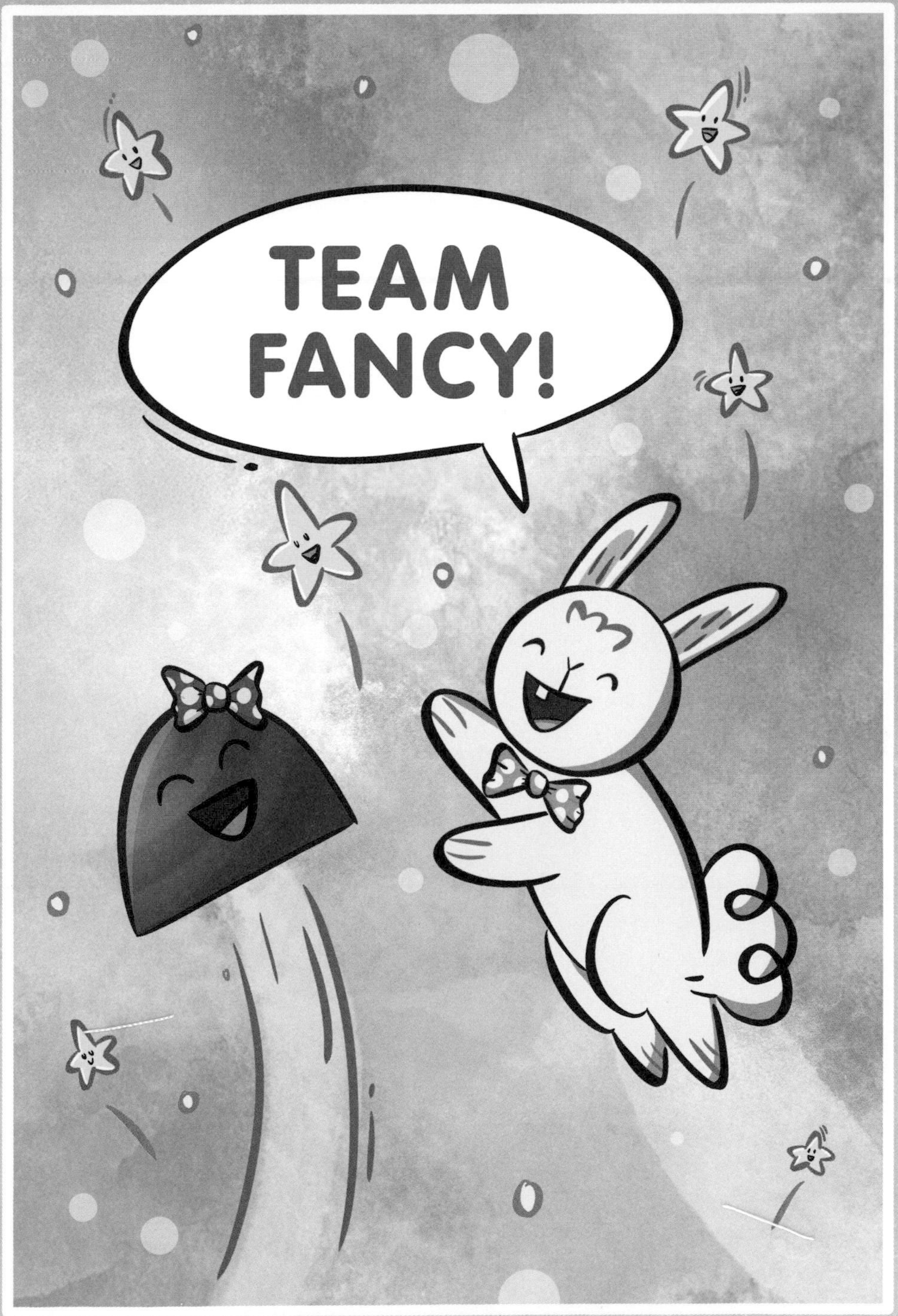
TEAM FANCY!

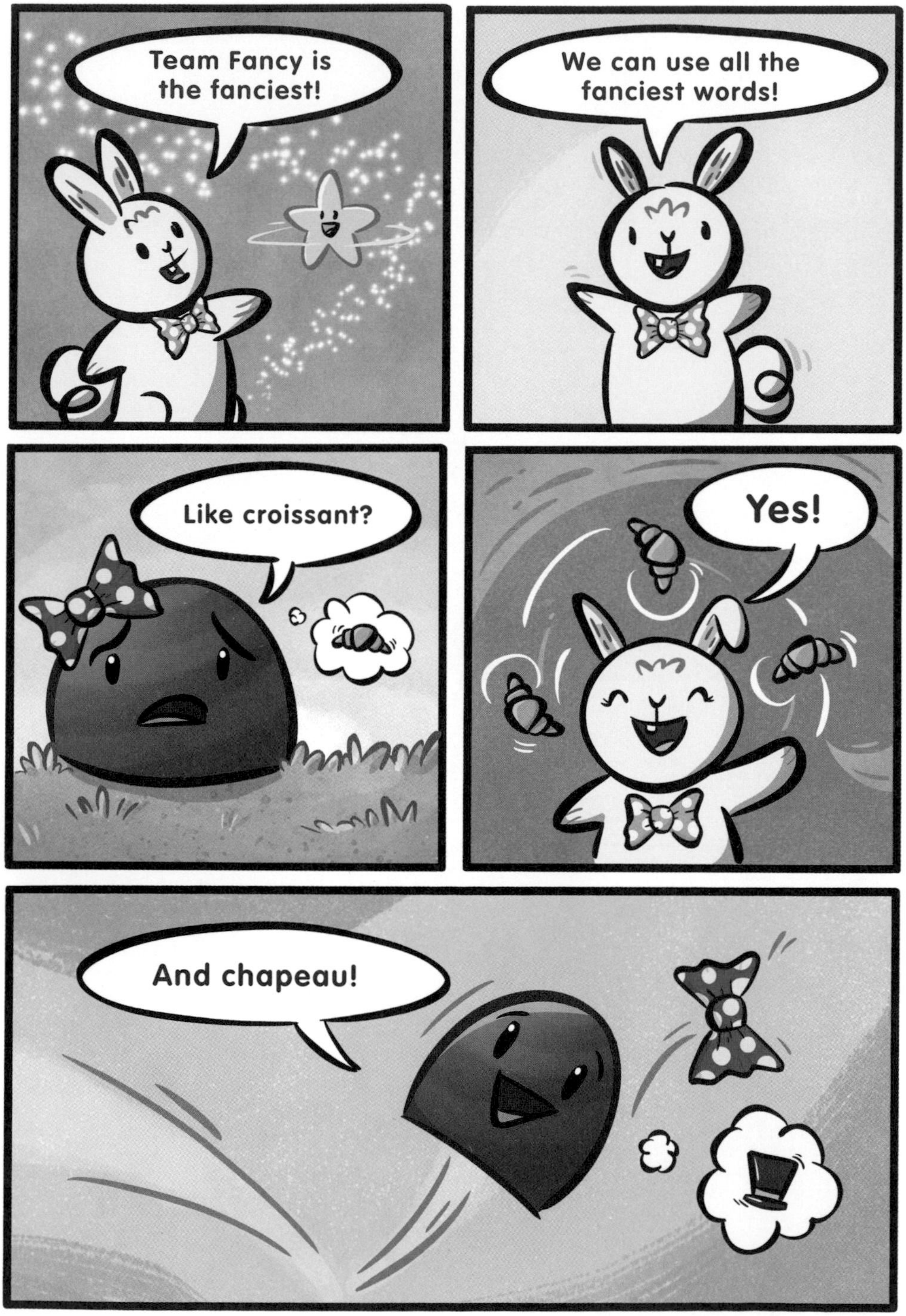
Team Fancy is the fanciest!
We can use all the fanciest words!
Like croissant?
Yes!
And chapeau!

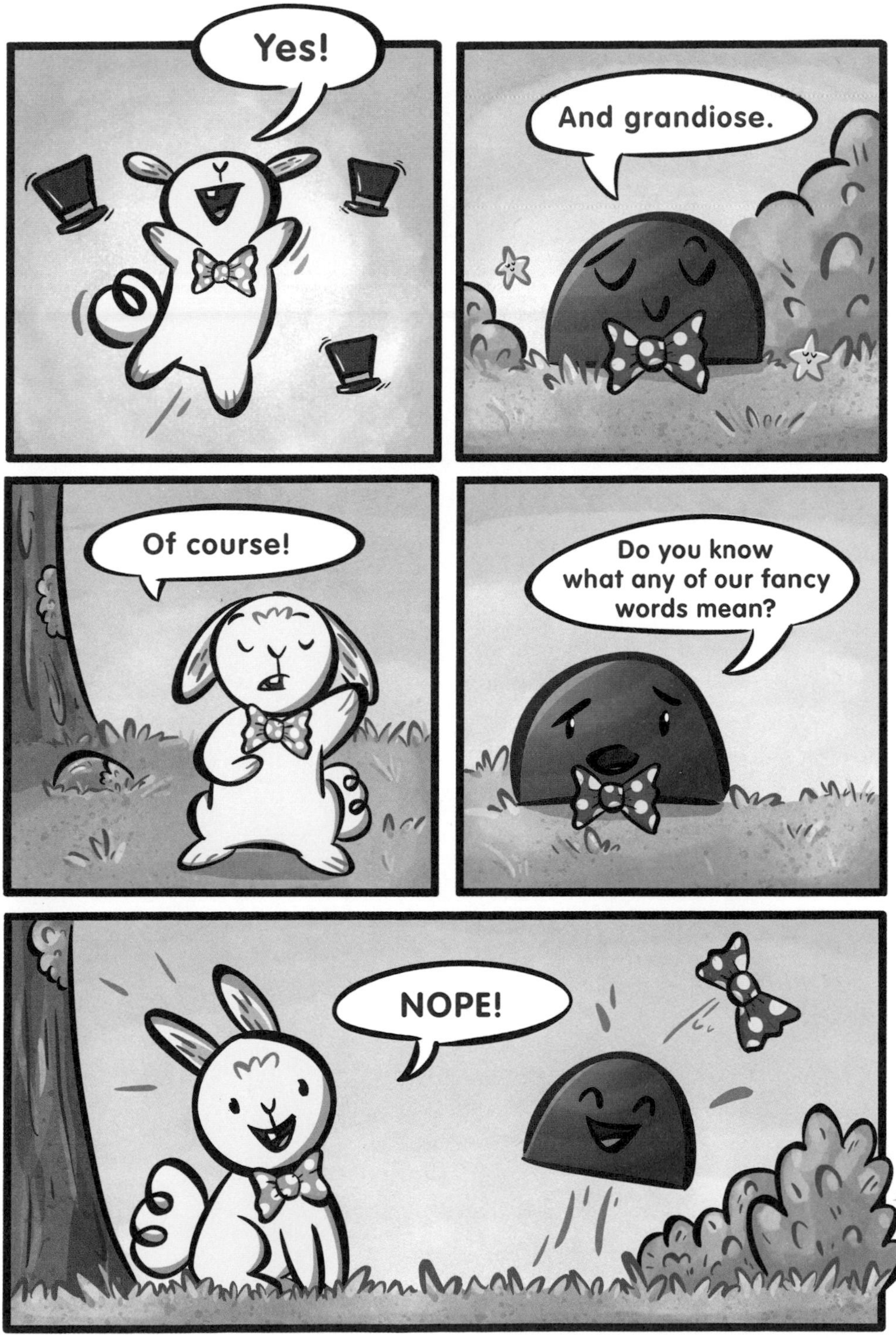
Yes!
And grandiose.
Of course!
Do you know what any of our fancy words mean?
NOPE!

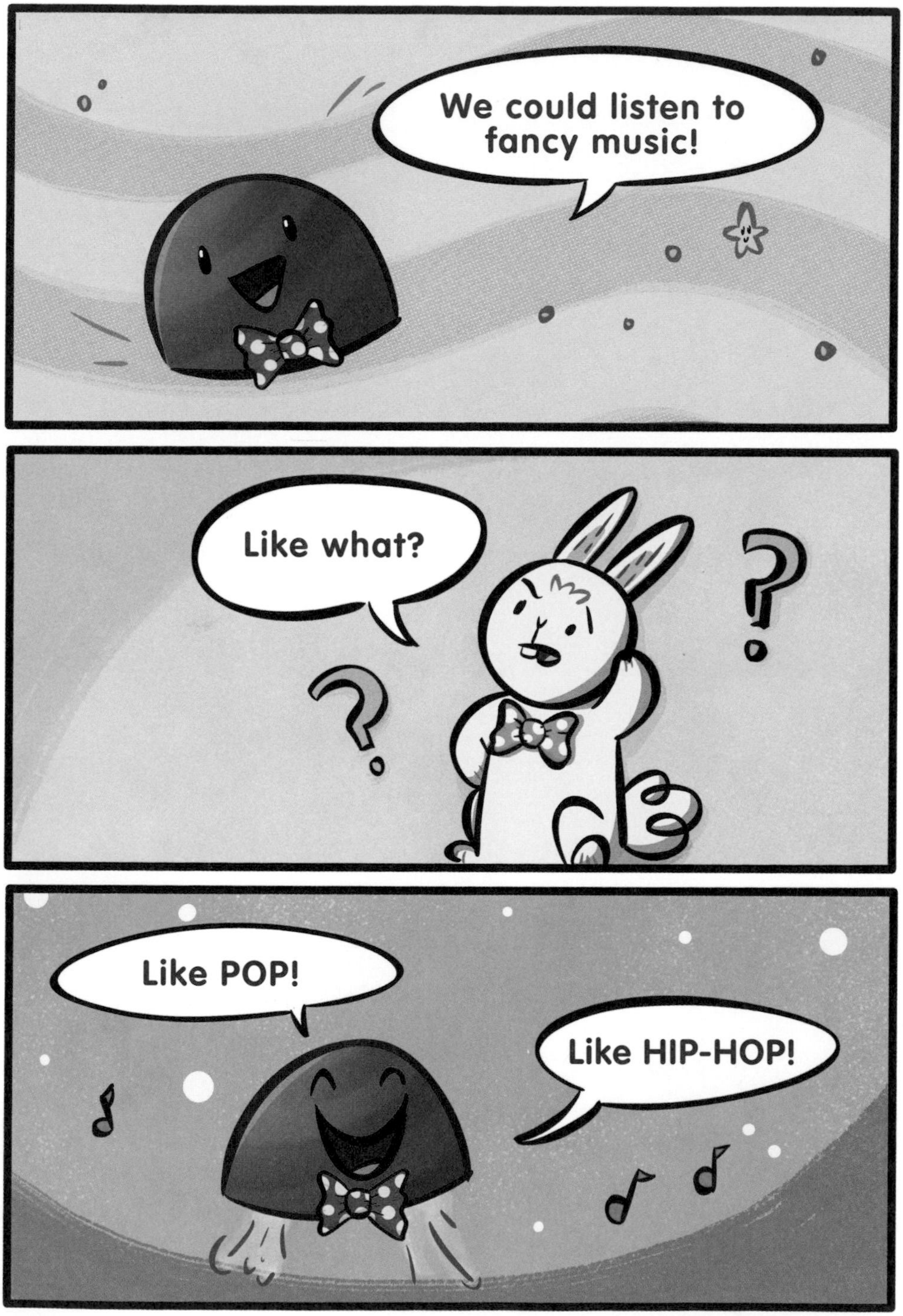
We could listen to fancy music!
Like what?
Like POP!
Like HIP-HOP!

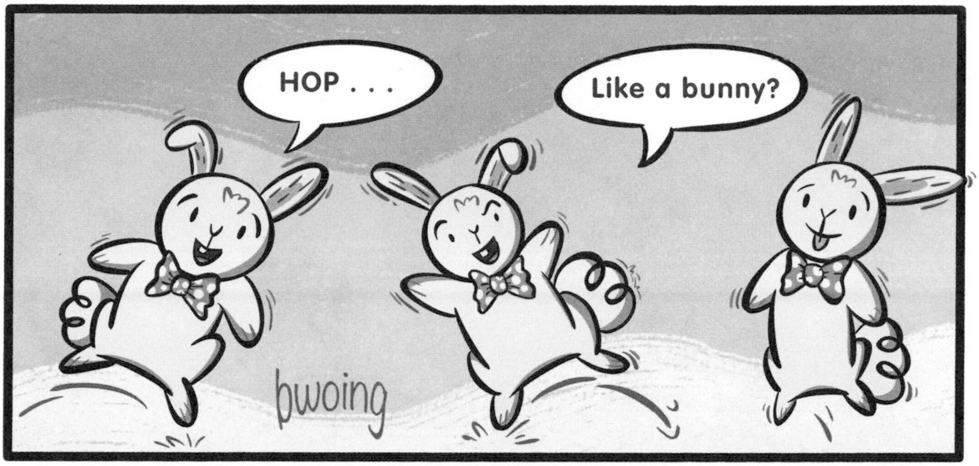
HOP . . .
Like a bunny?
bwoing

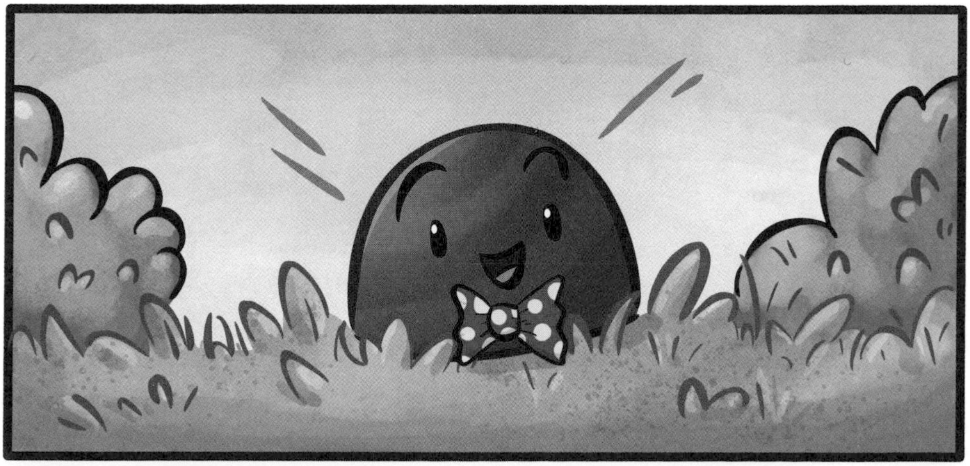

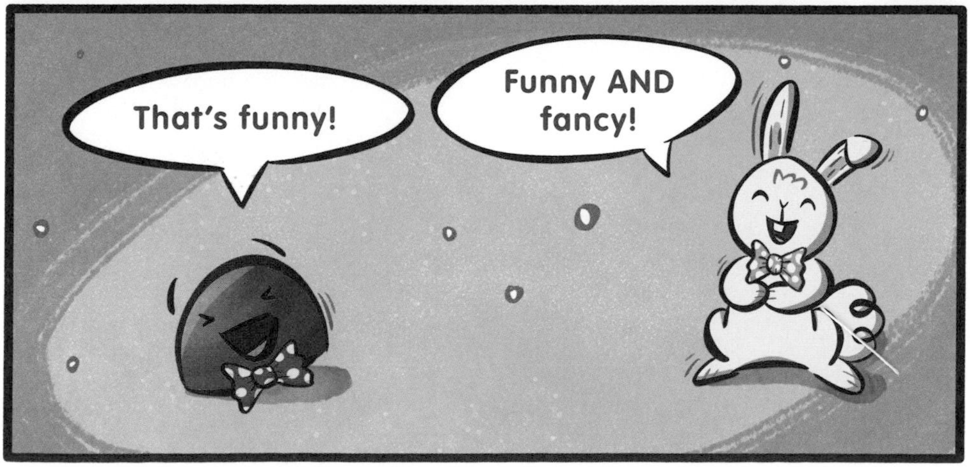
That's funny!
Funny AND fancy!

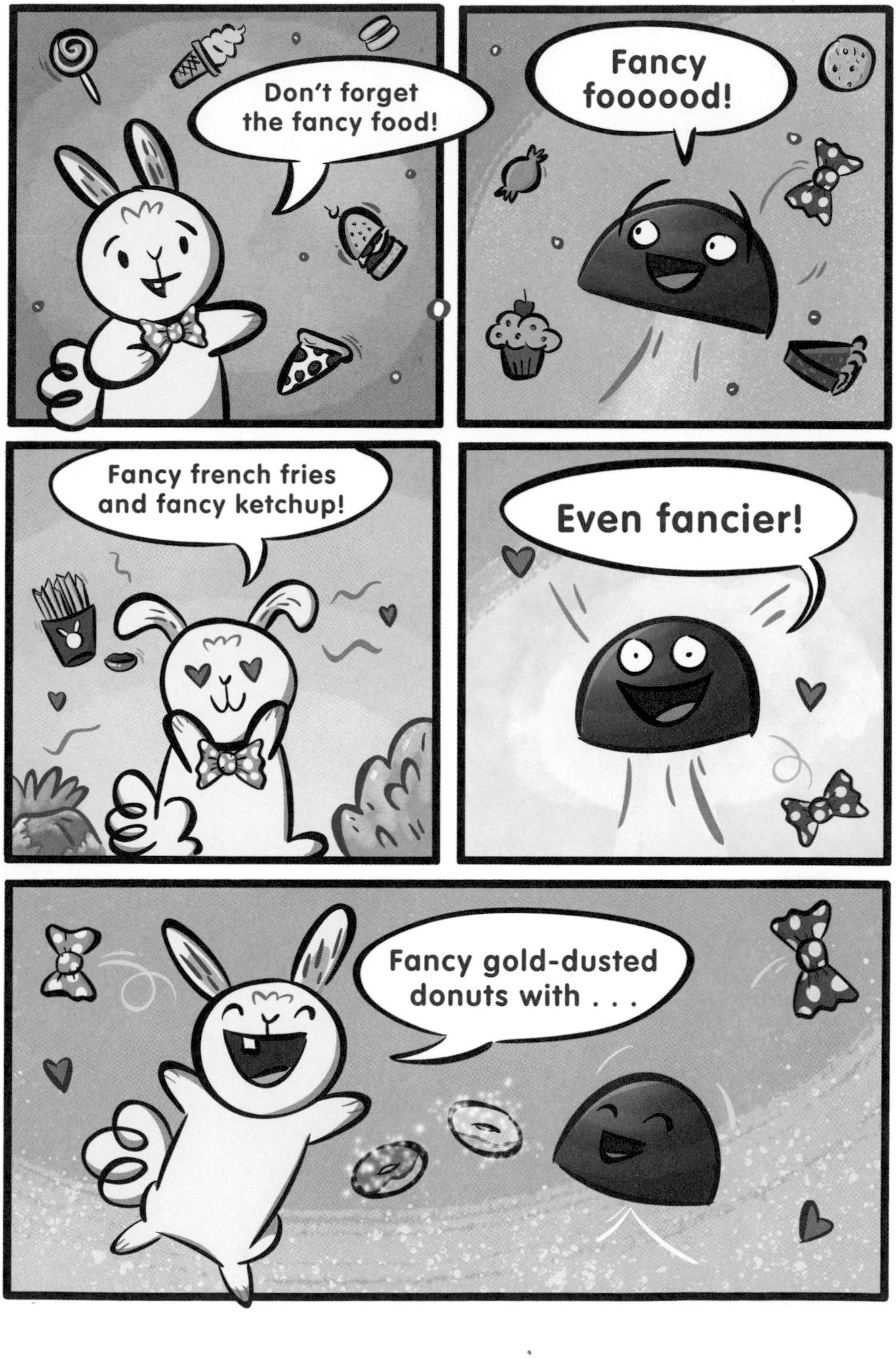
Don't forget the fancy food!
Fancy fooooood!
Fancy french fries and fancy ketchup!
Even fancier!
Fancy gold-dusted donuts with . . .

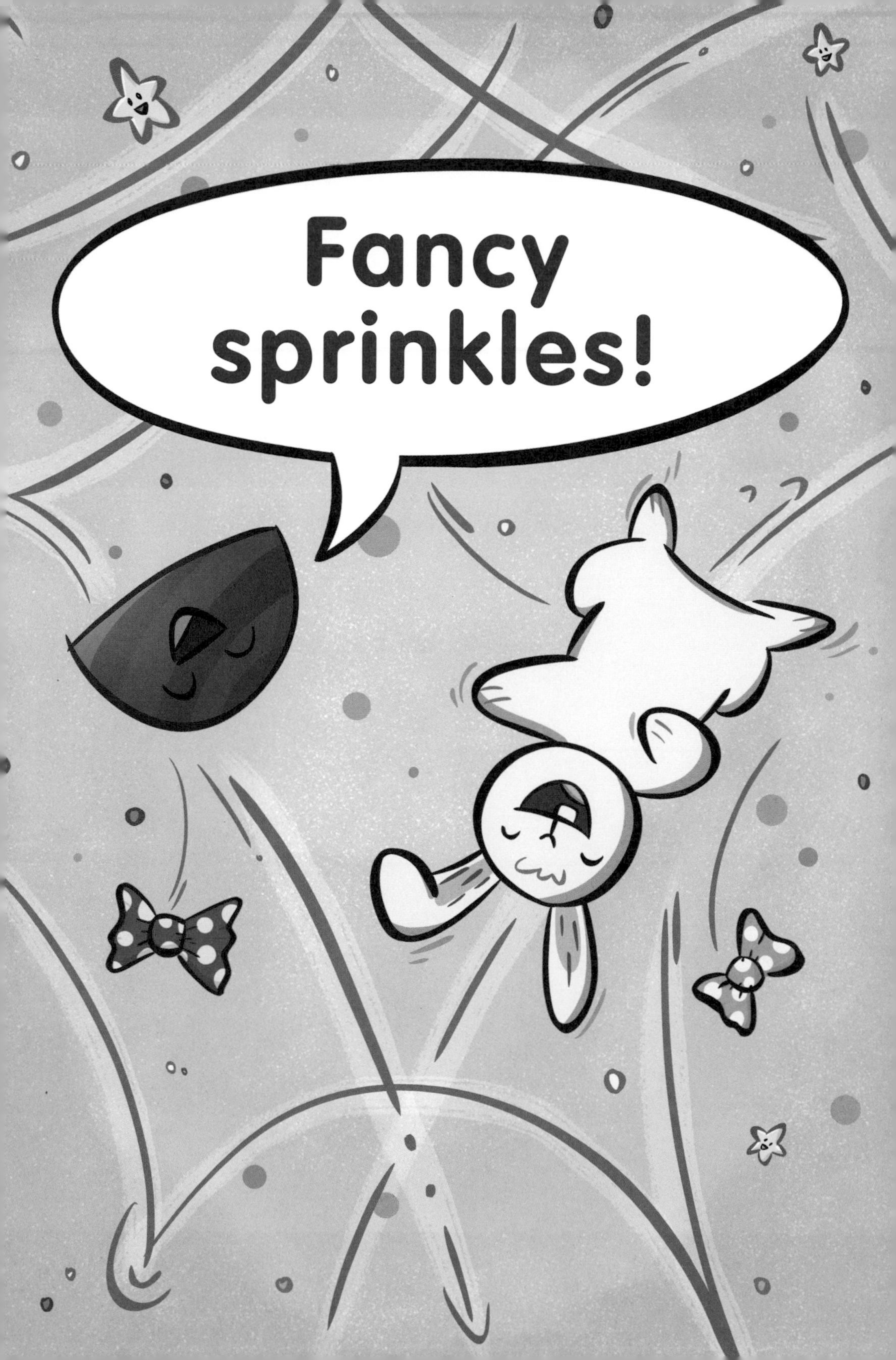
Fancy sprinkles!

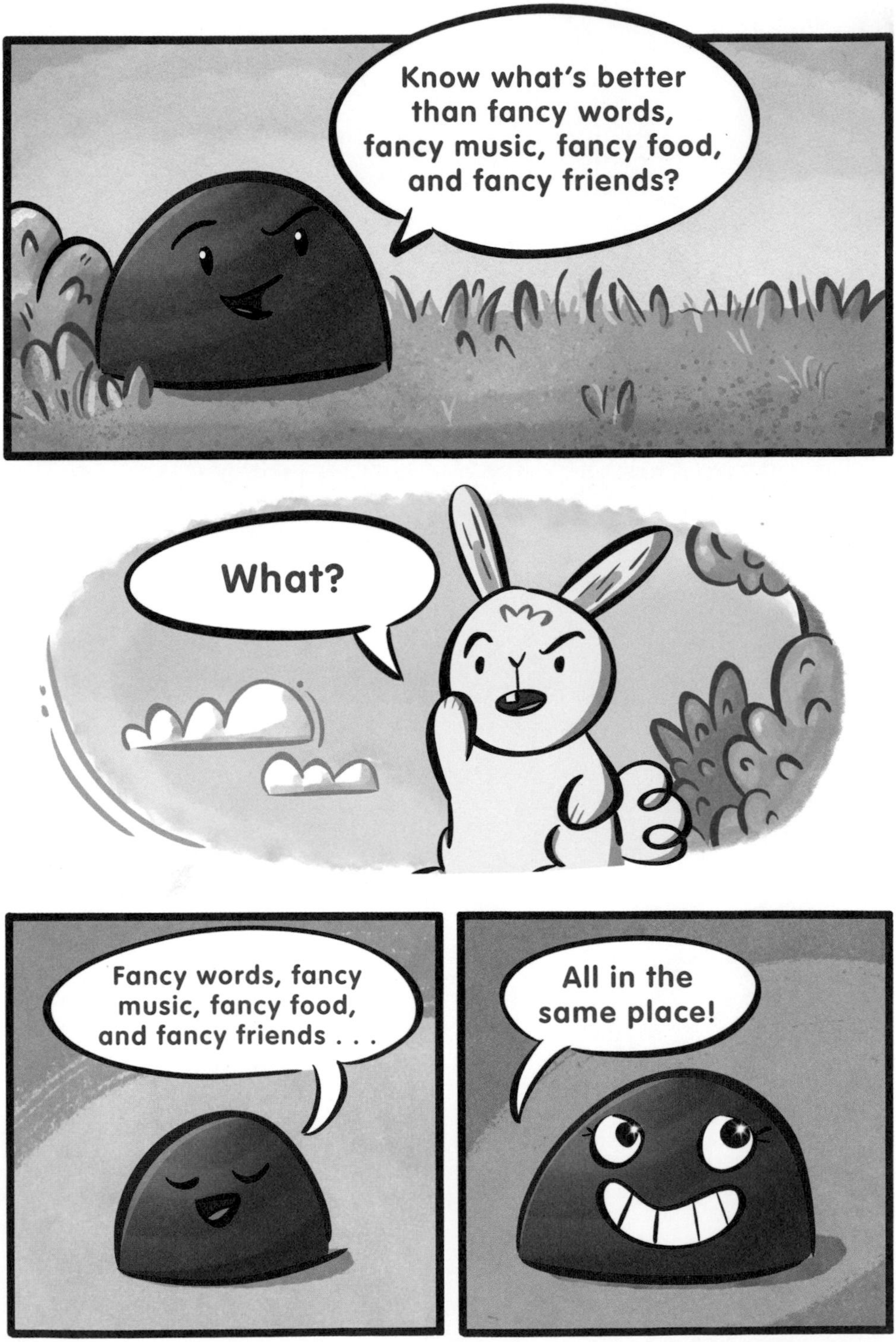
Know what's better than fancy words, fancy music, fancy food, and fancy friends?
What?
Fancy words, fancy music, fancy food, and fancy friends . . .
All in the same place!

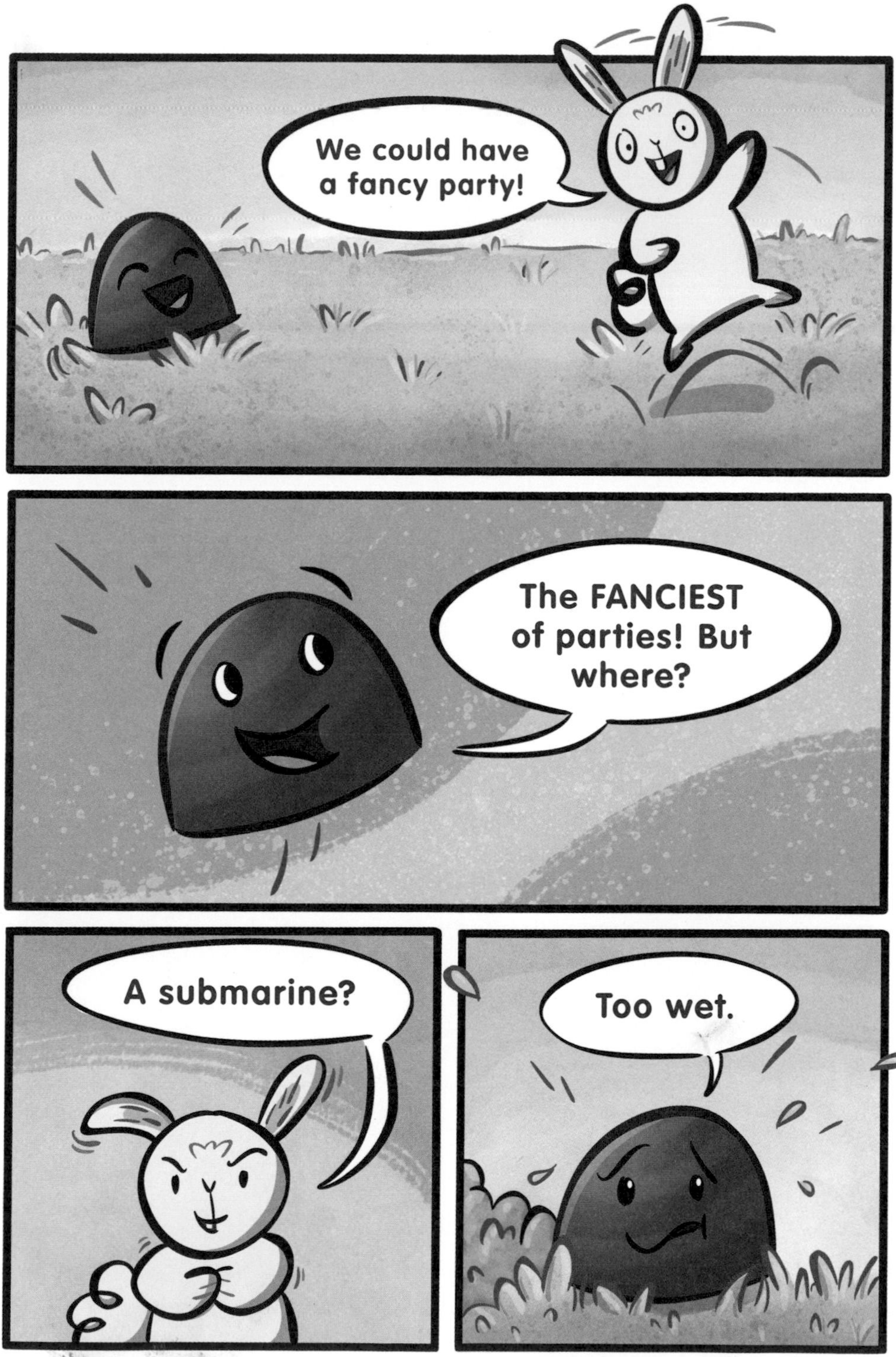
We could have a fancy party!
The FANCIEST of parties! But where?
A submarine?
Too wet.

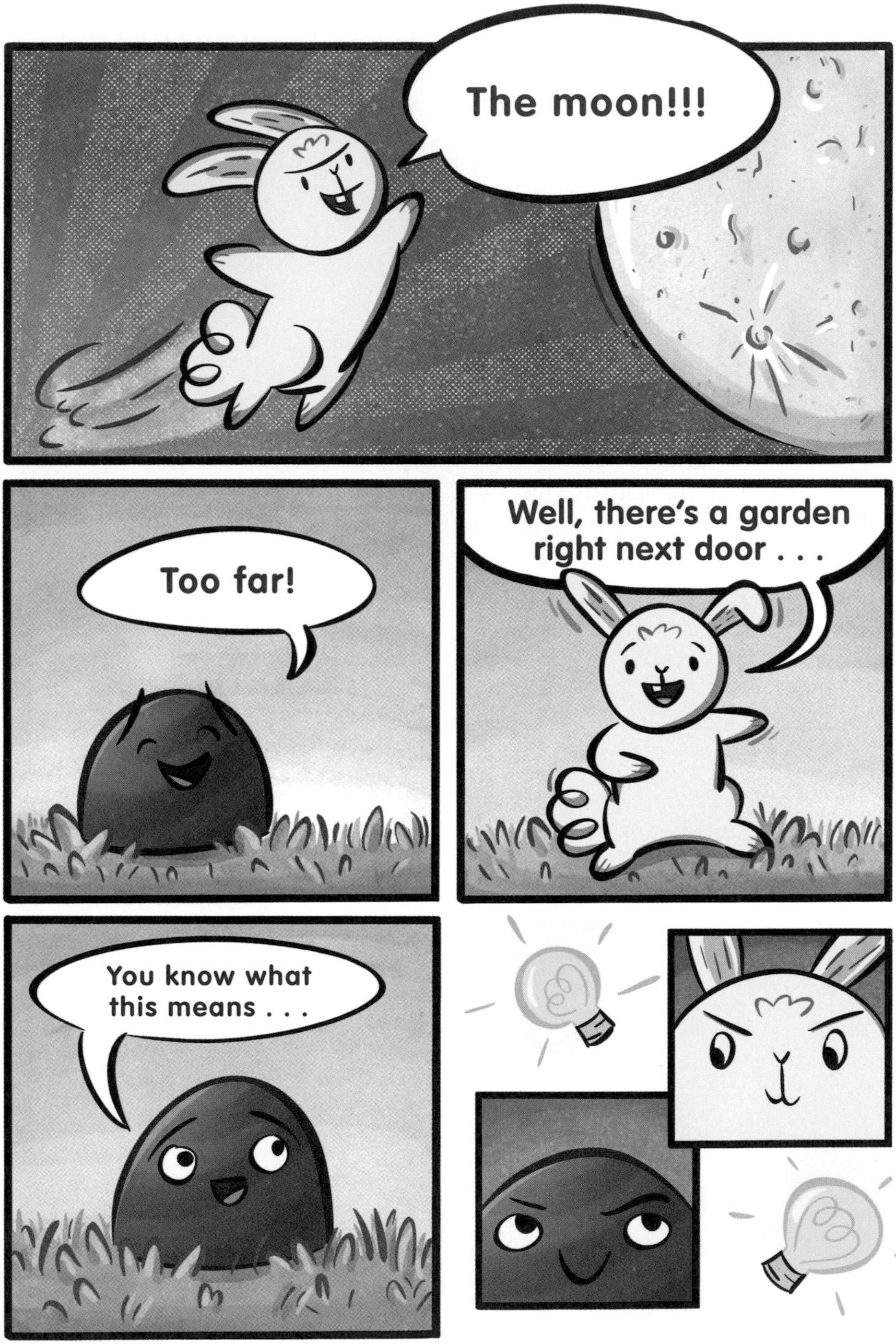
The moon!!!
Too far!
Well, there's a garden
right next door . . .
You know what
this means . . .

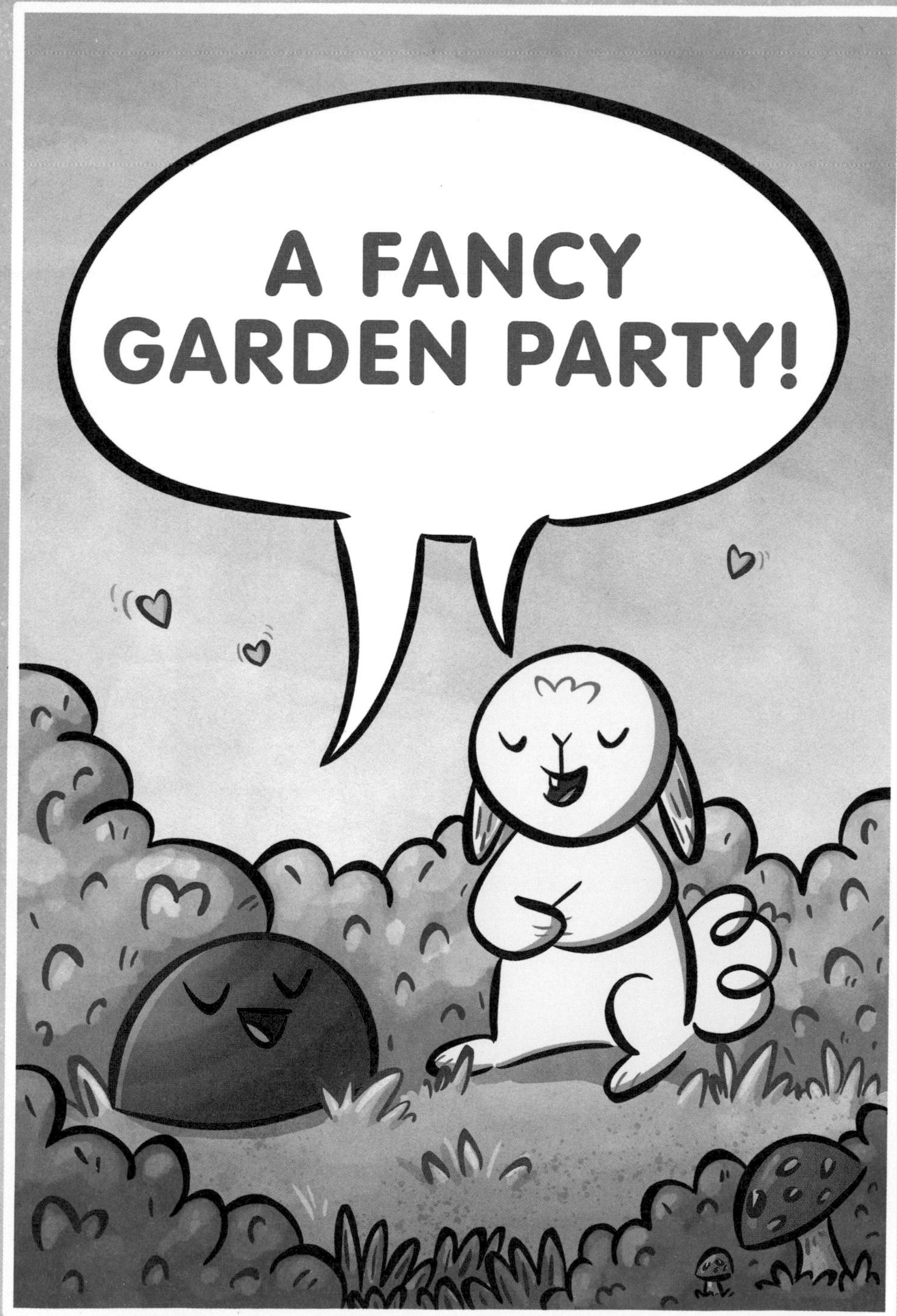
A FANCY GARDEN PARTY!

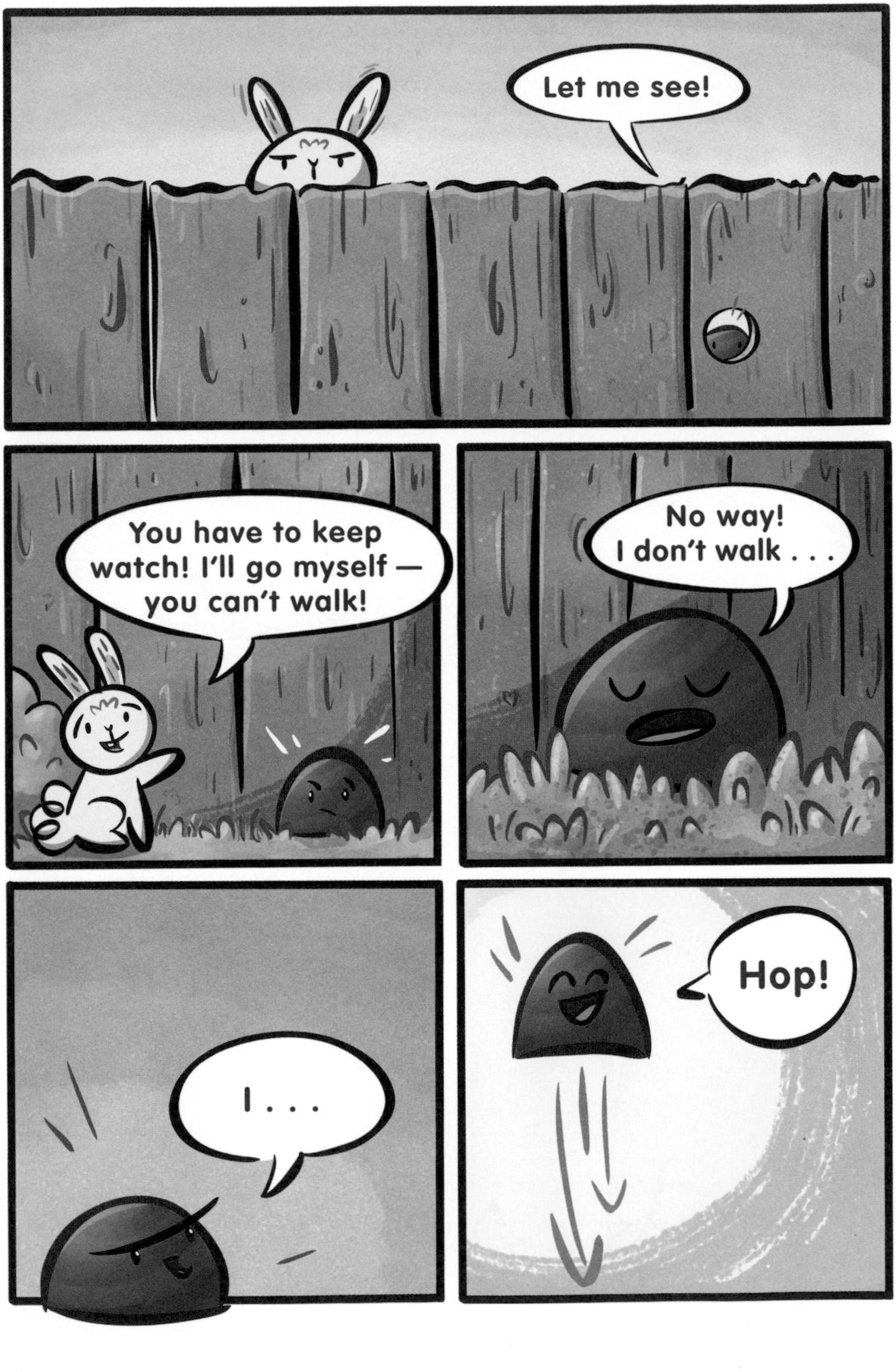
Let me see!
You have to keep watch! I'll go myself — you can't walk!
No way! I don't walk . . .
I . . .
Hop!

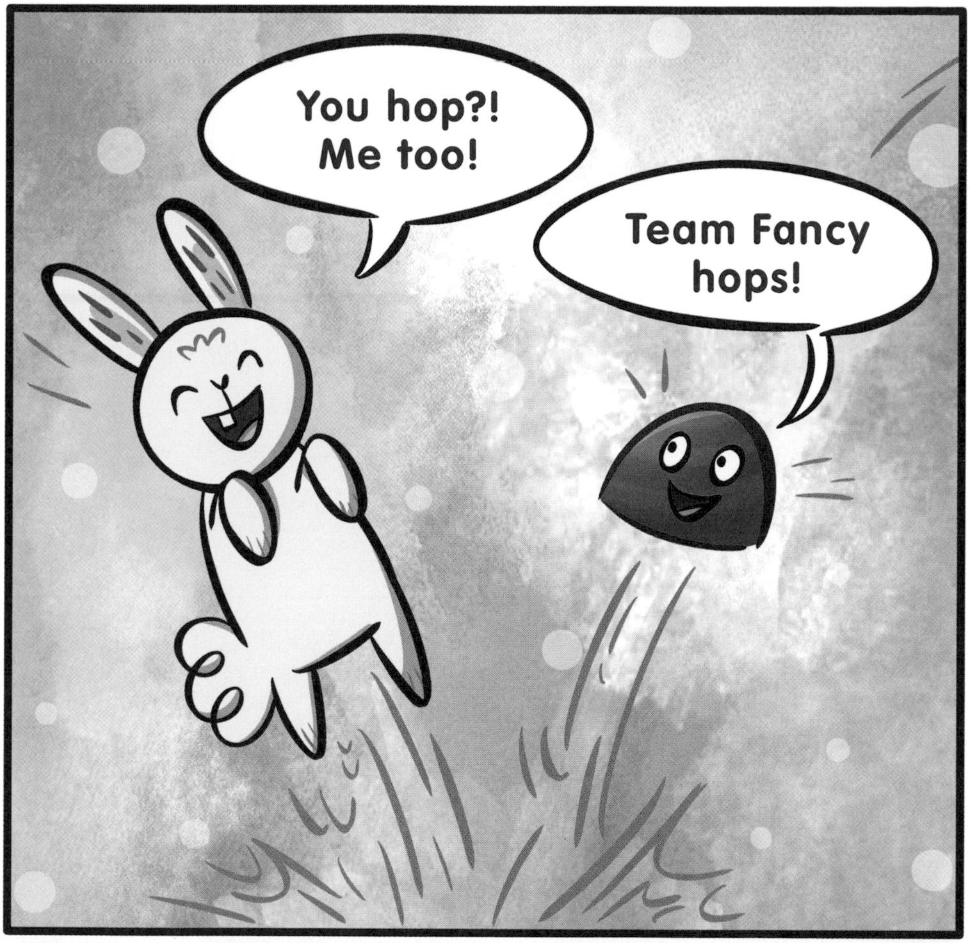
You hop?! Me too!
Team Fancy hops!

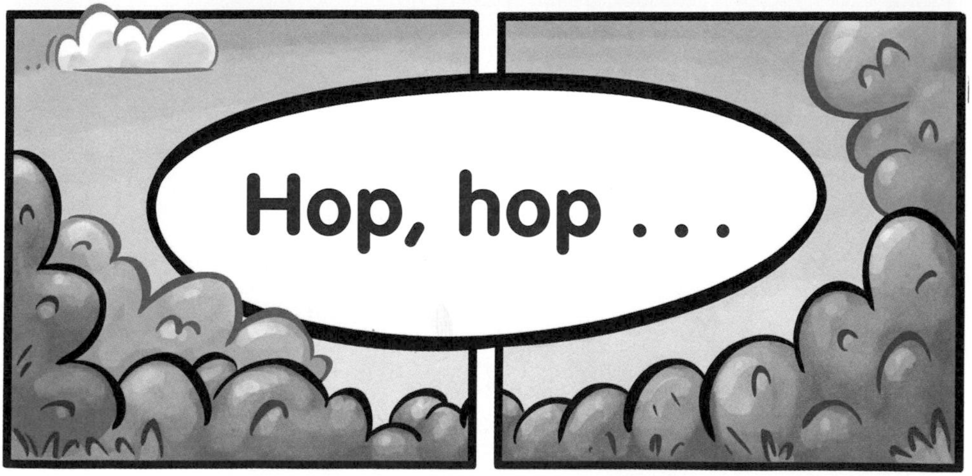
Hop, hop . . .

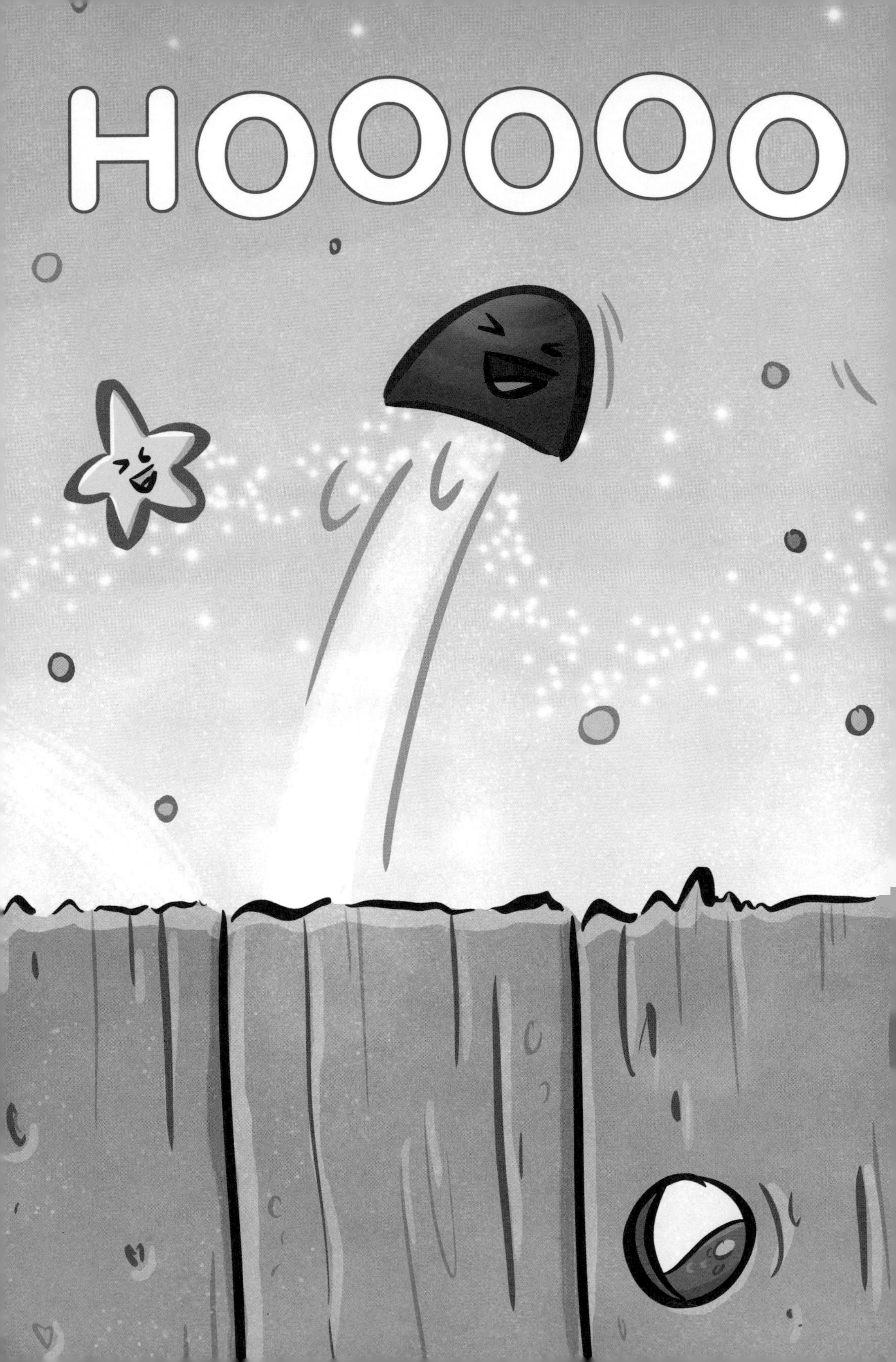
HOOOOO

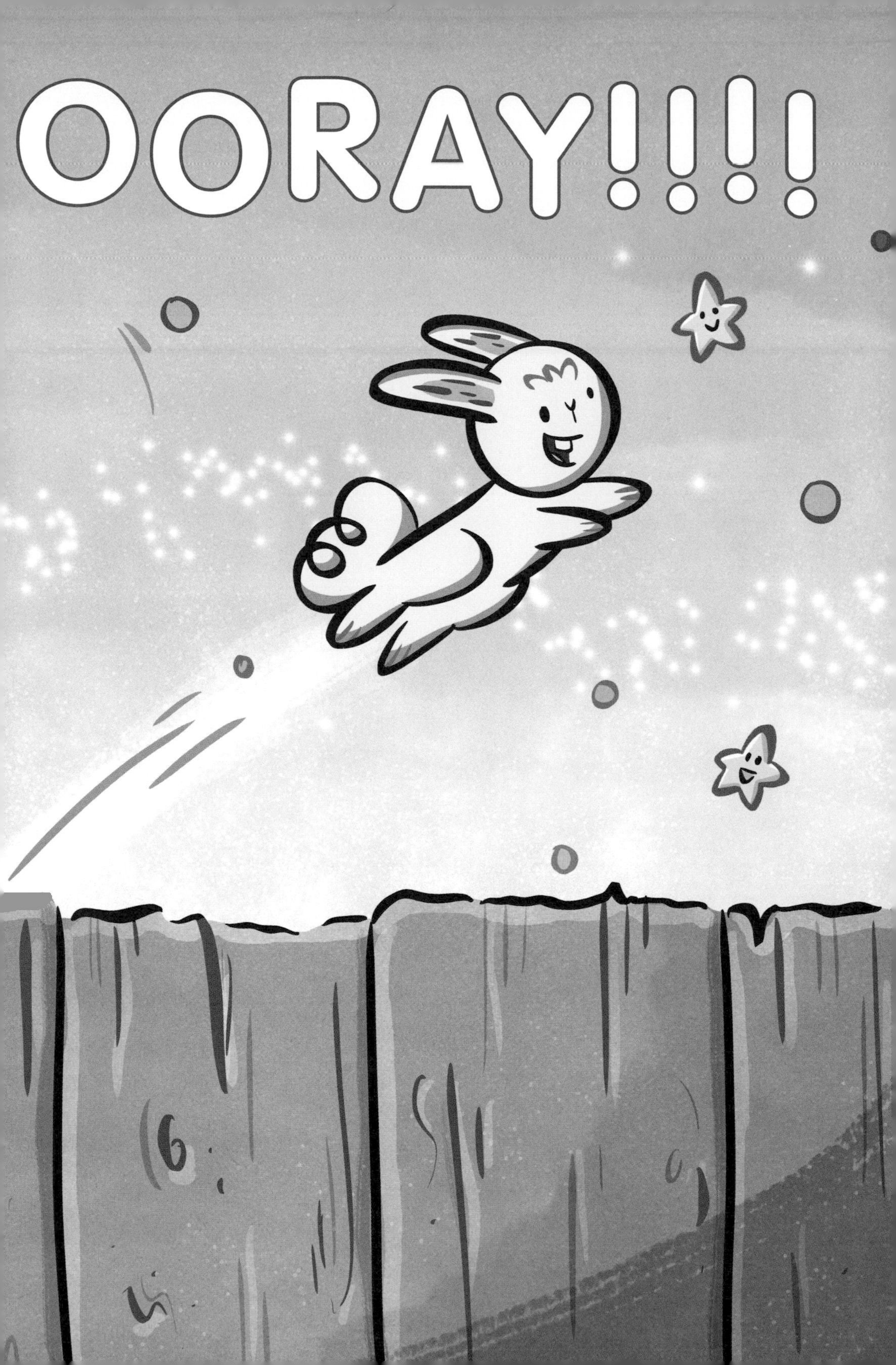
OORAY!!!!

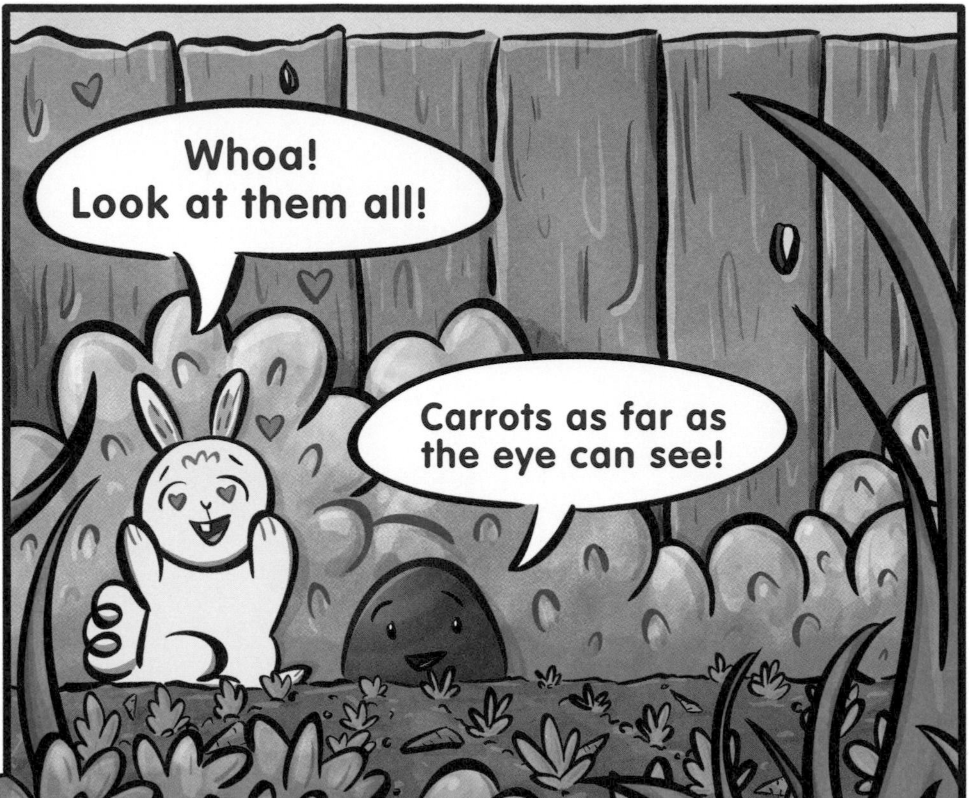
Whoa!
Look at them all!
Carrots as far as the eye can see!

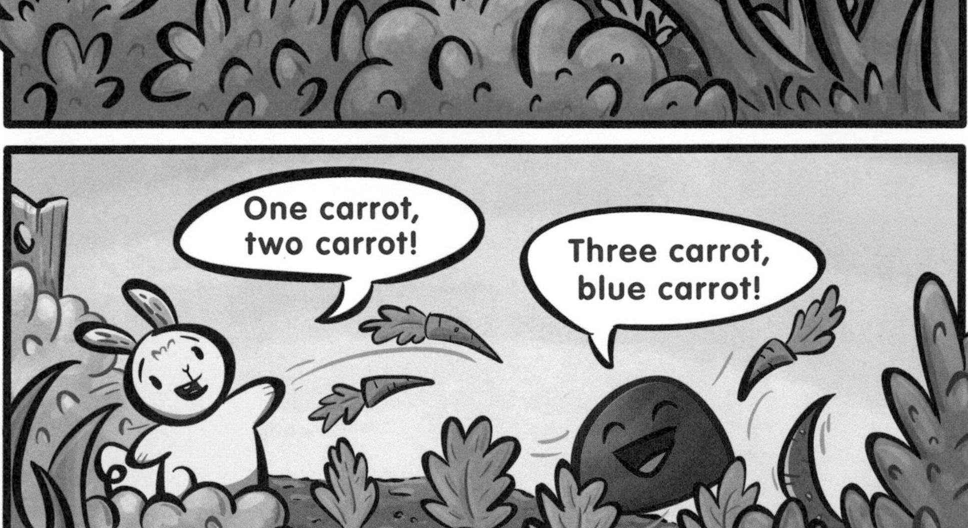
One carrot, two carrot!
Three carrot, blue carrot!

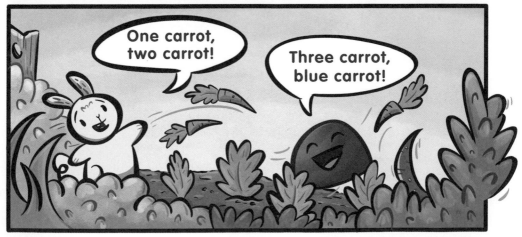

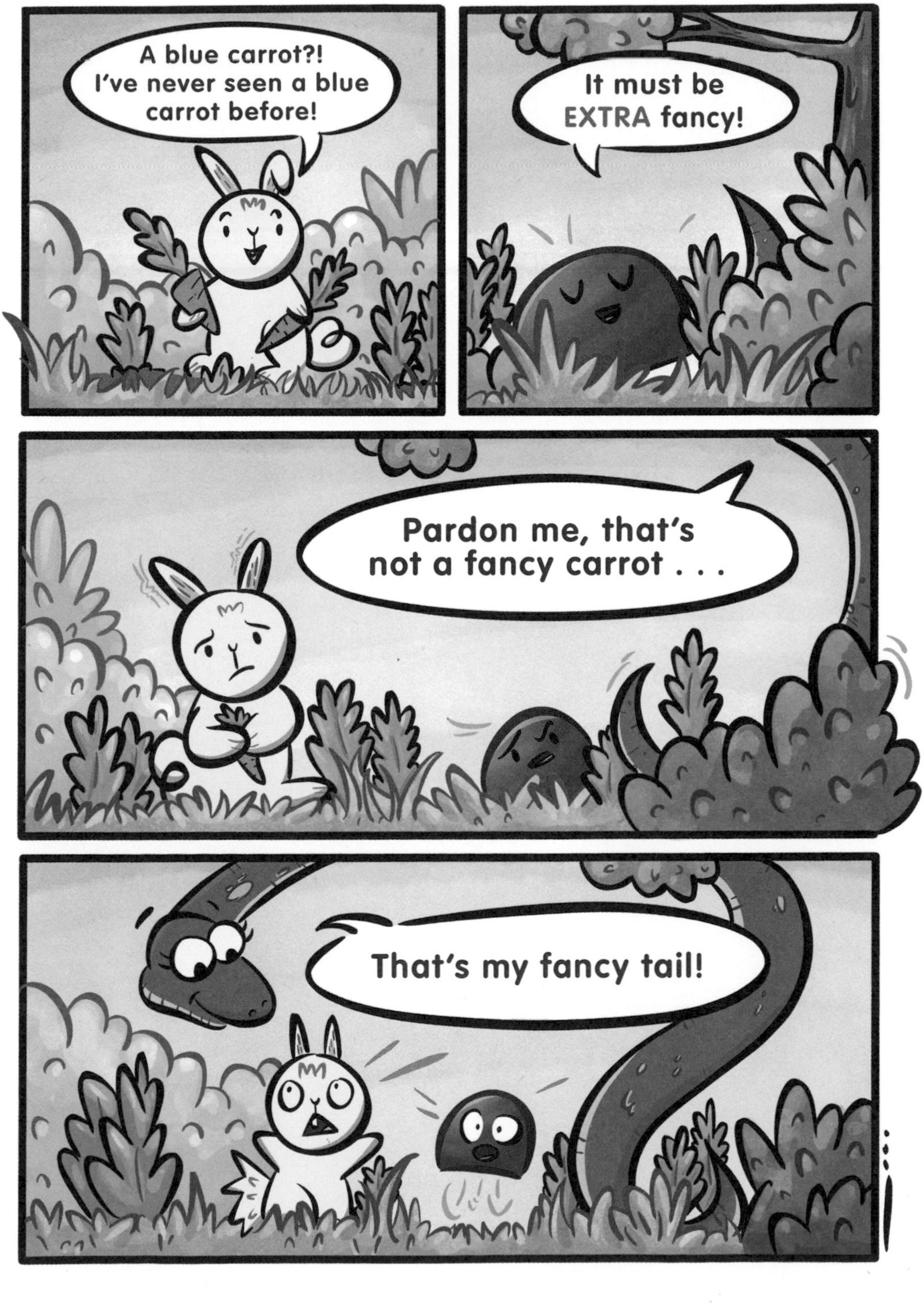
A blue carrot?! I've never seen a blue carrot before!
It must be EXTRA fancy!
Pardon me, that's not a fancy carrot . . .
That's my fancy tail!

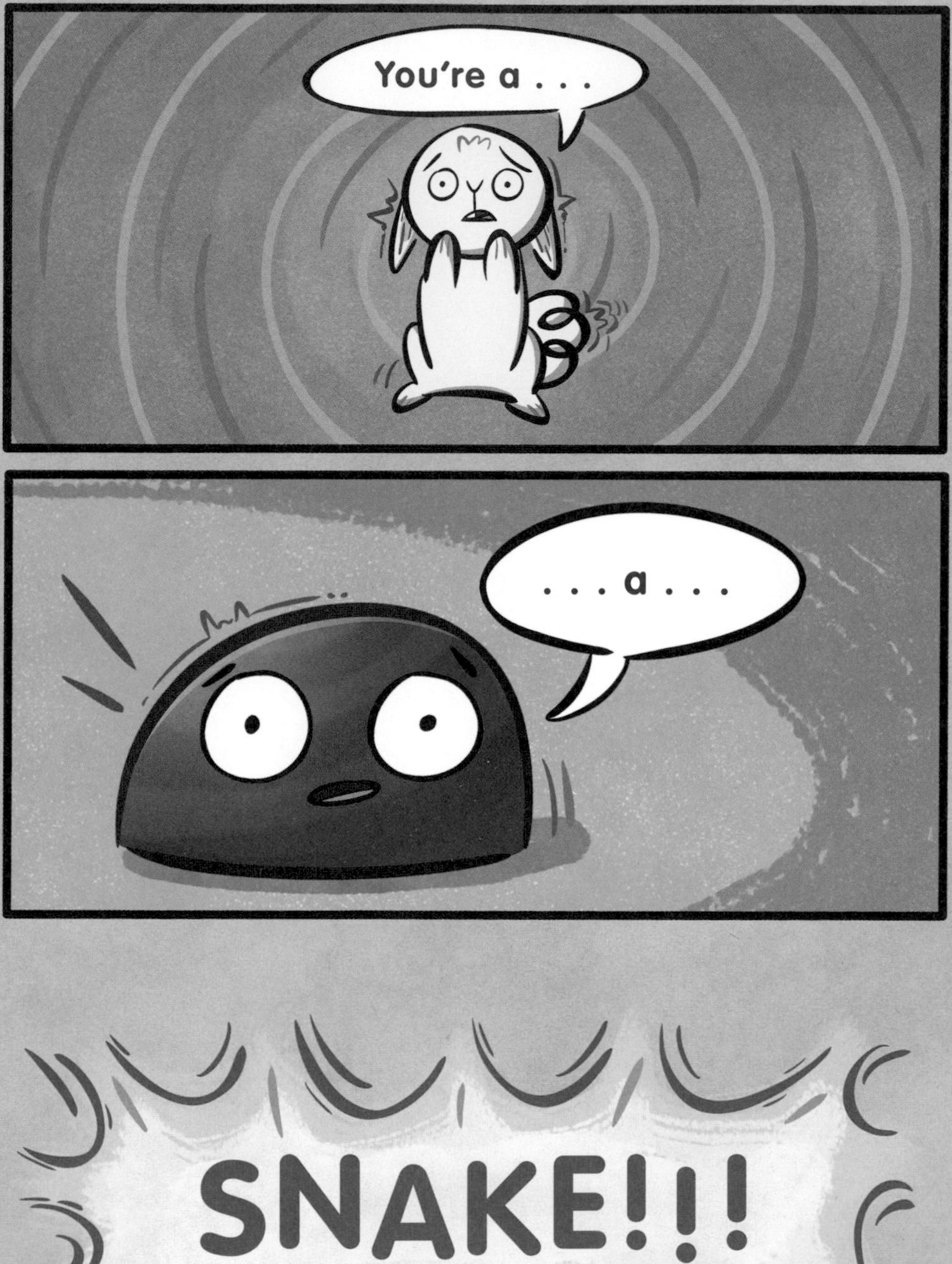
You're a . . .
. . . a . . .
SNAKE!!!

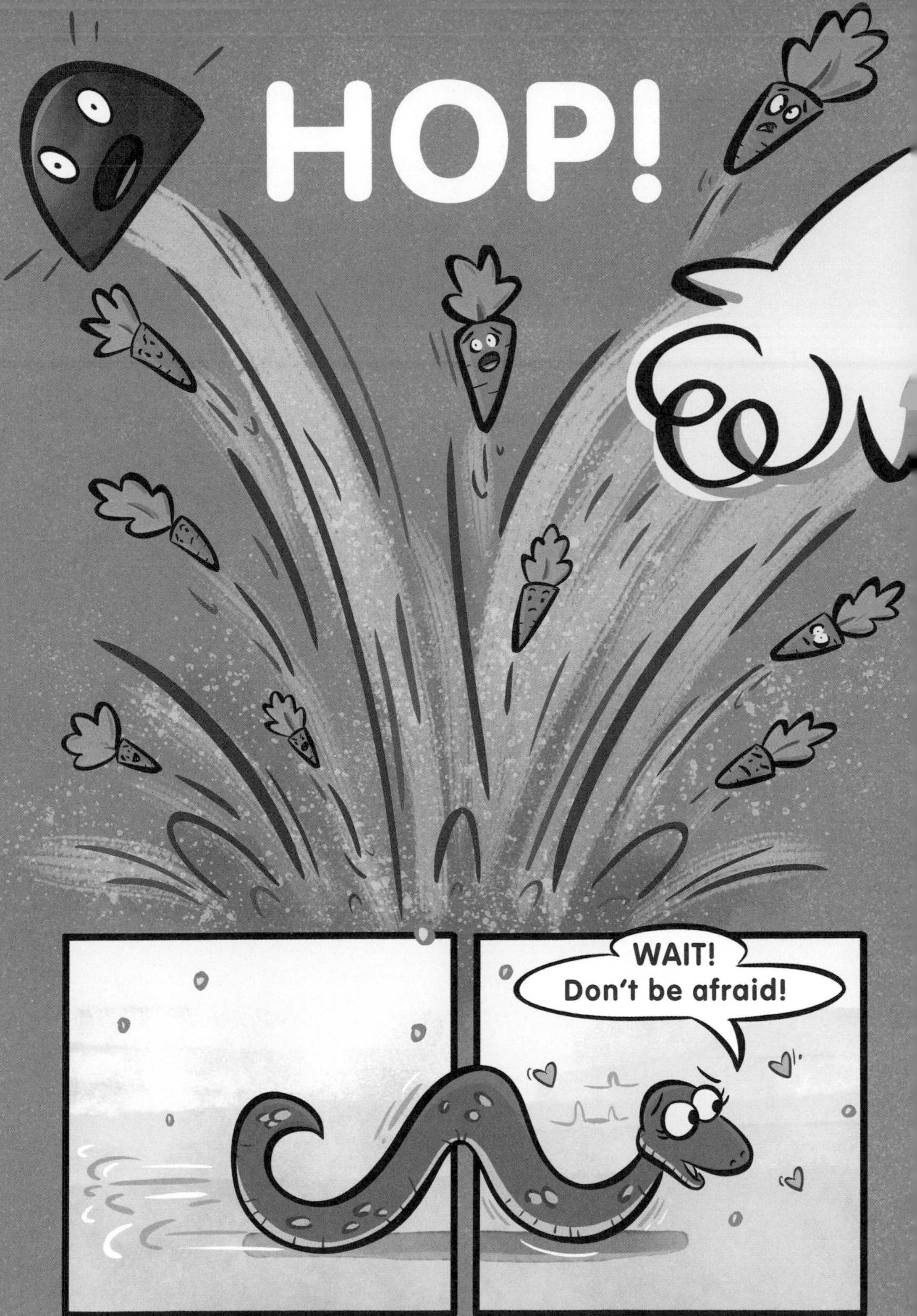
HOP!
WAIT!
Don't be afraid!

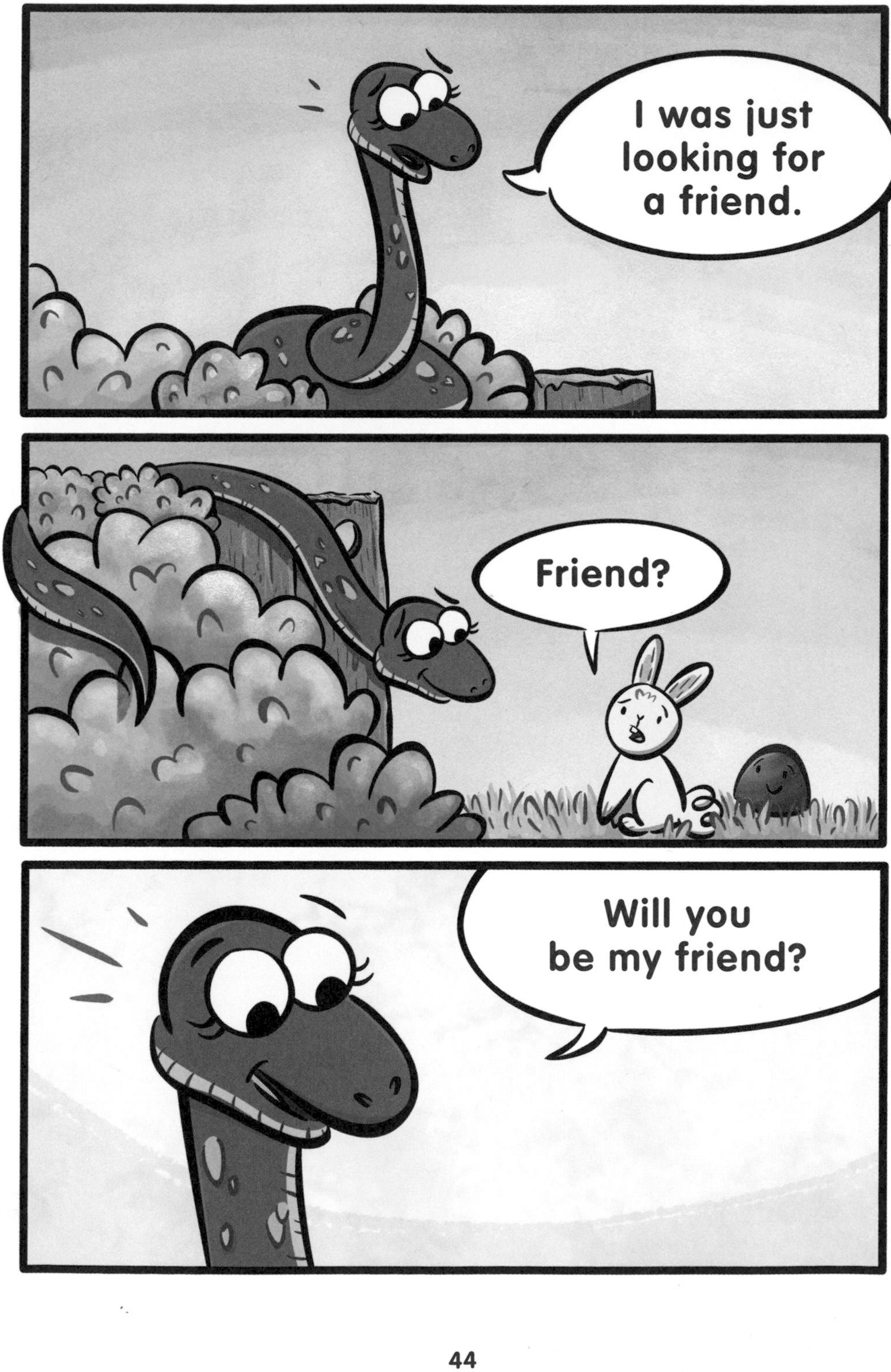
I was just looking for a friend.
Friend?
Will you be my friend?

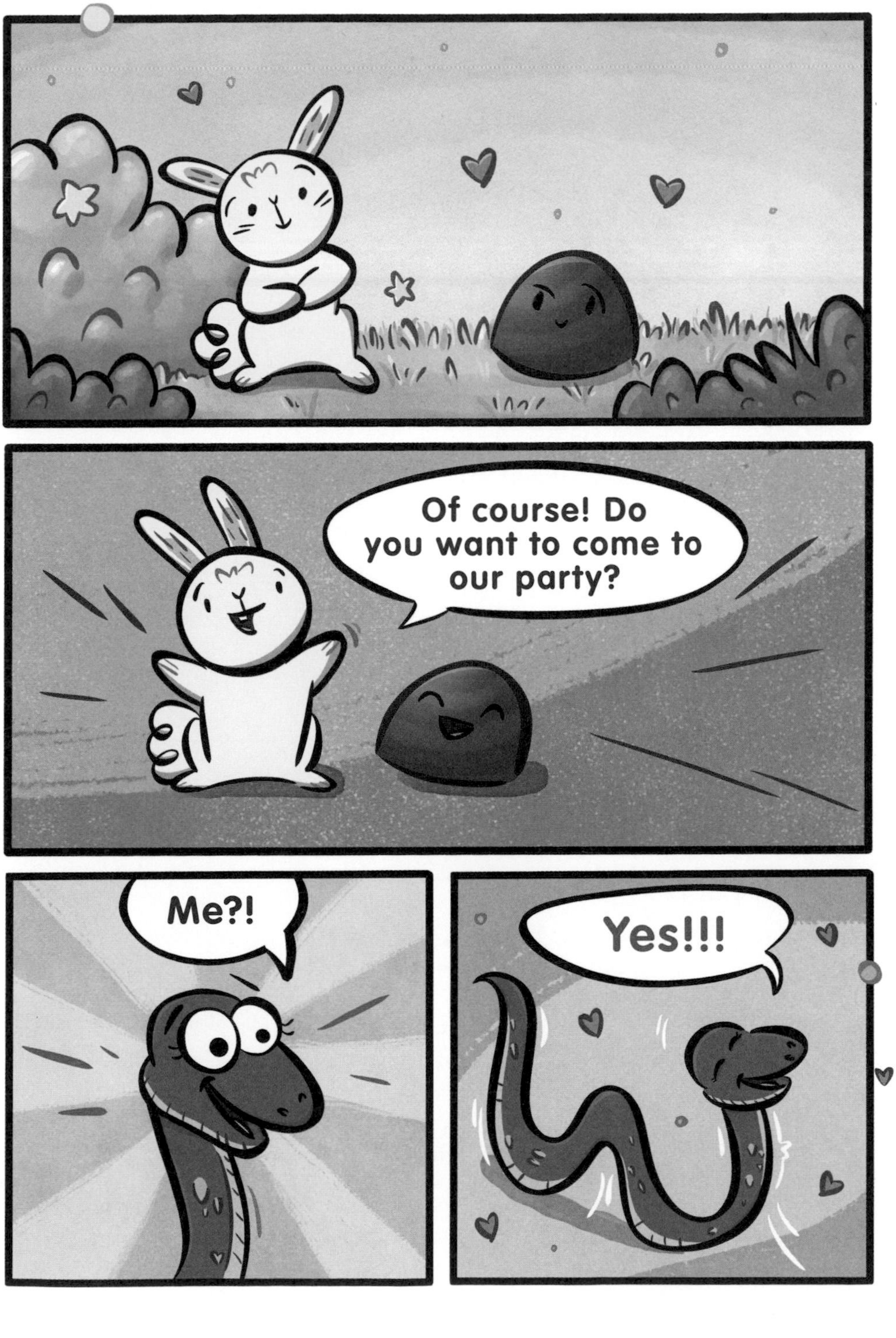
Of course! Do you want to come to our party?
Me?!
Yes!!!

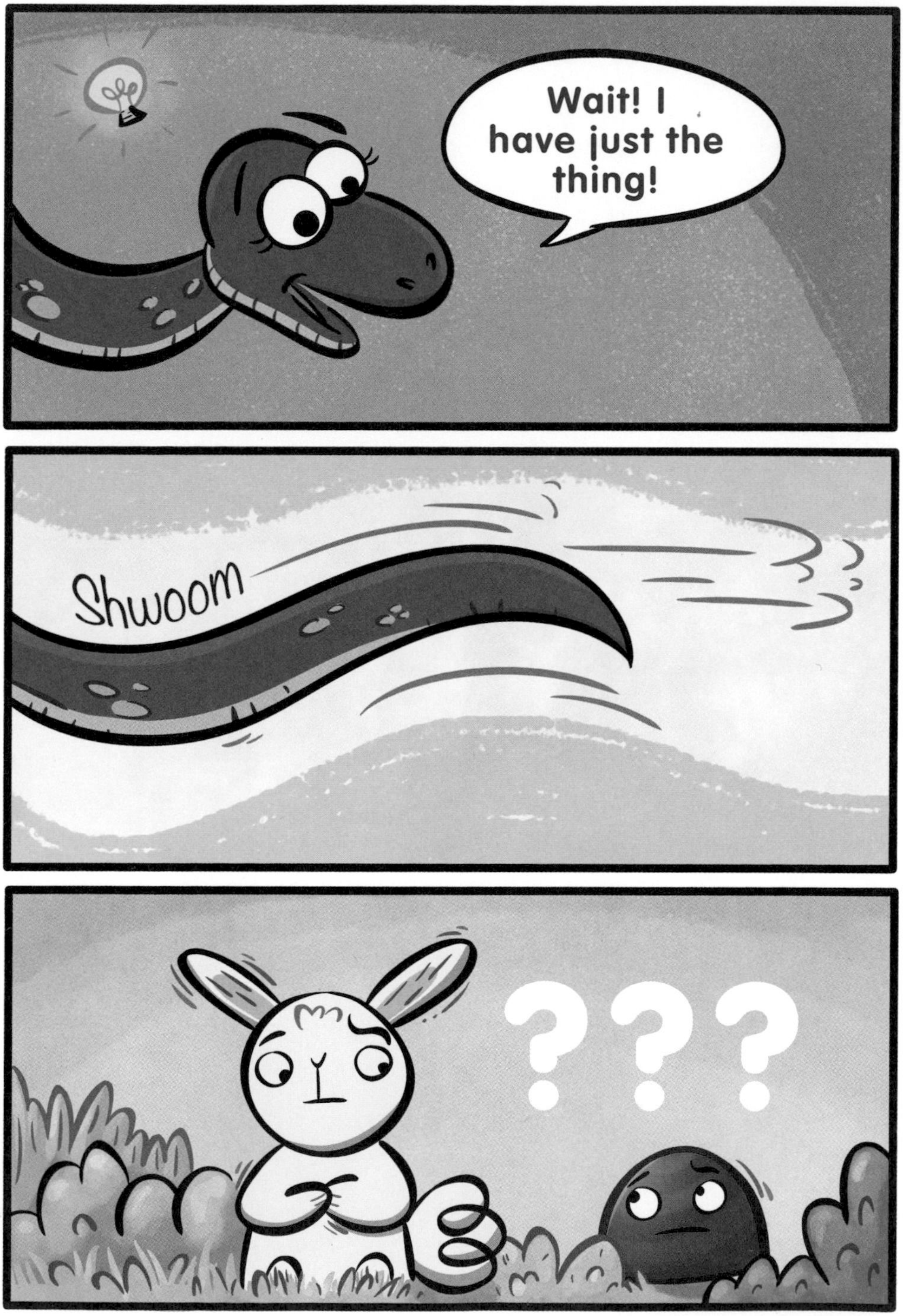

Wait! I have just the thing!
Shwoom
???

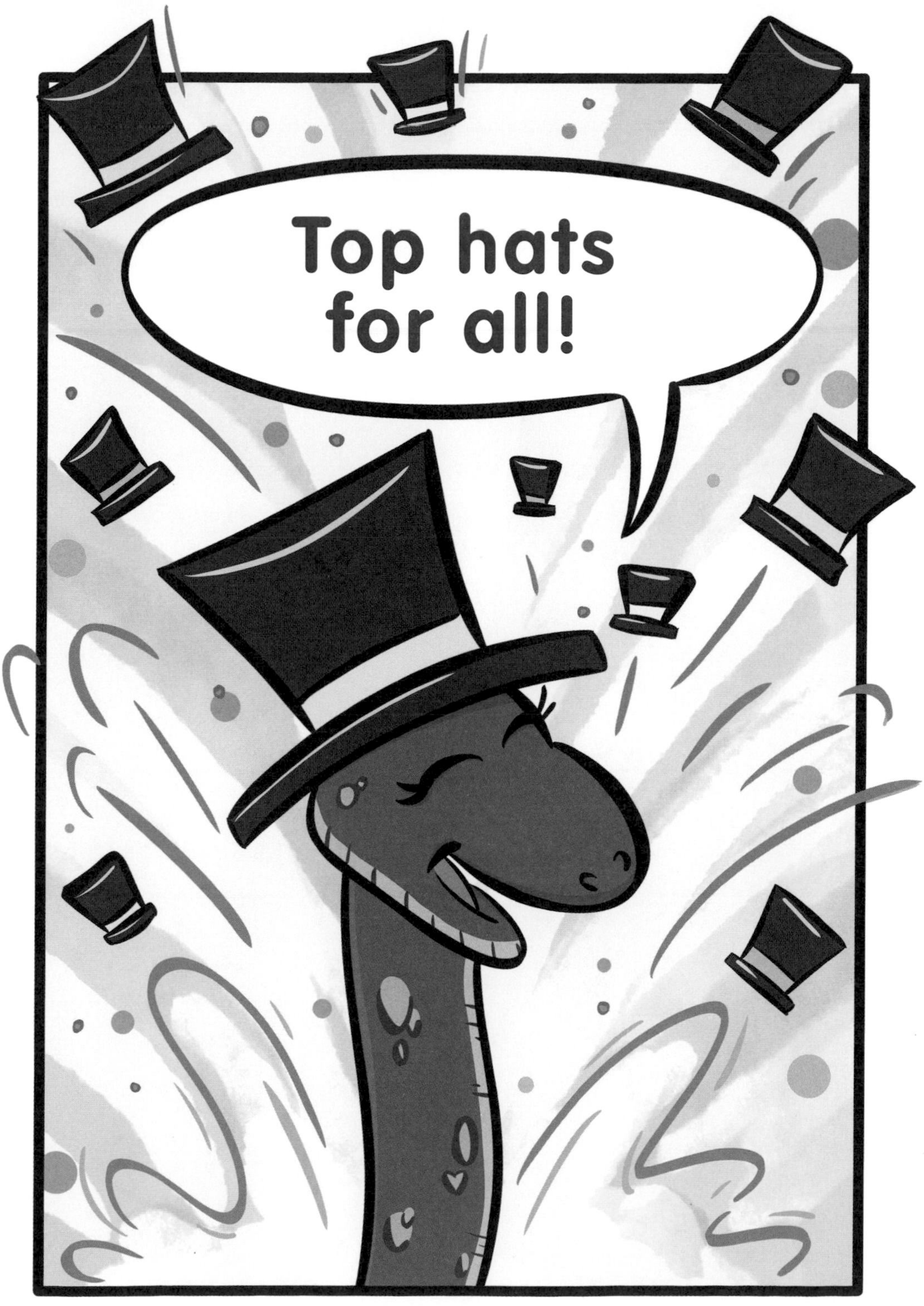
Top hats for all!

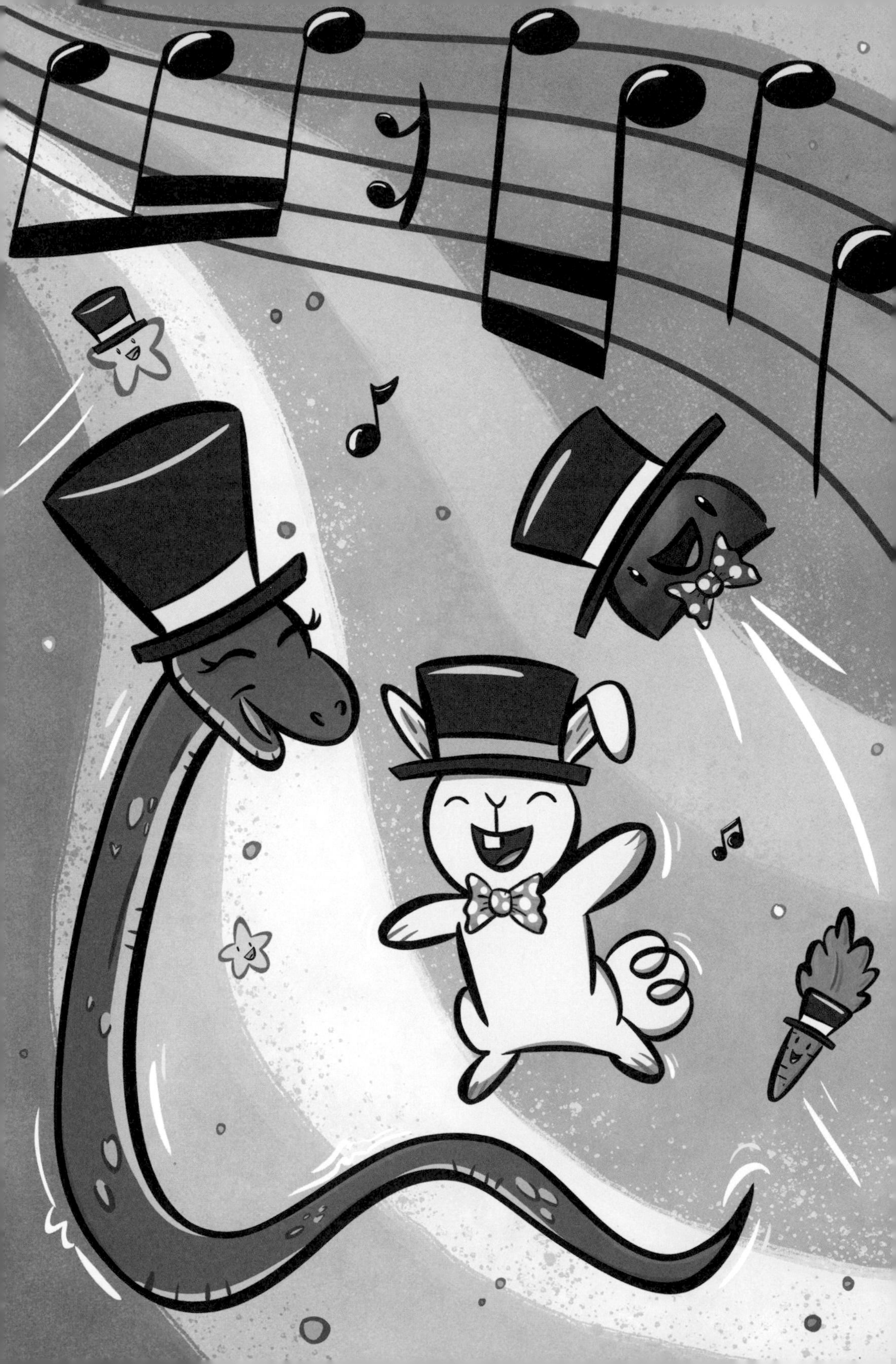

DONUTS
FOR LUNCH!

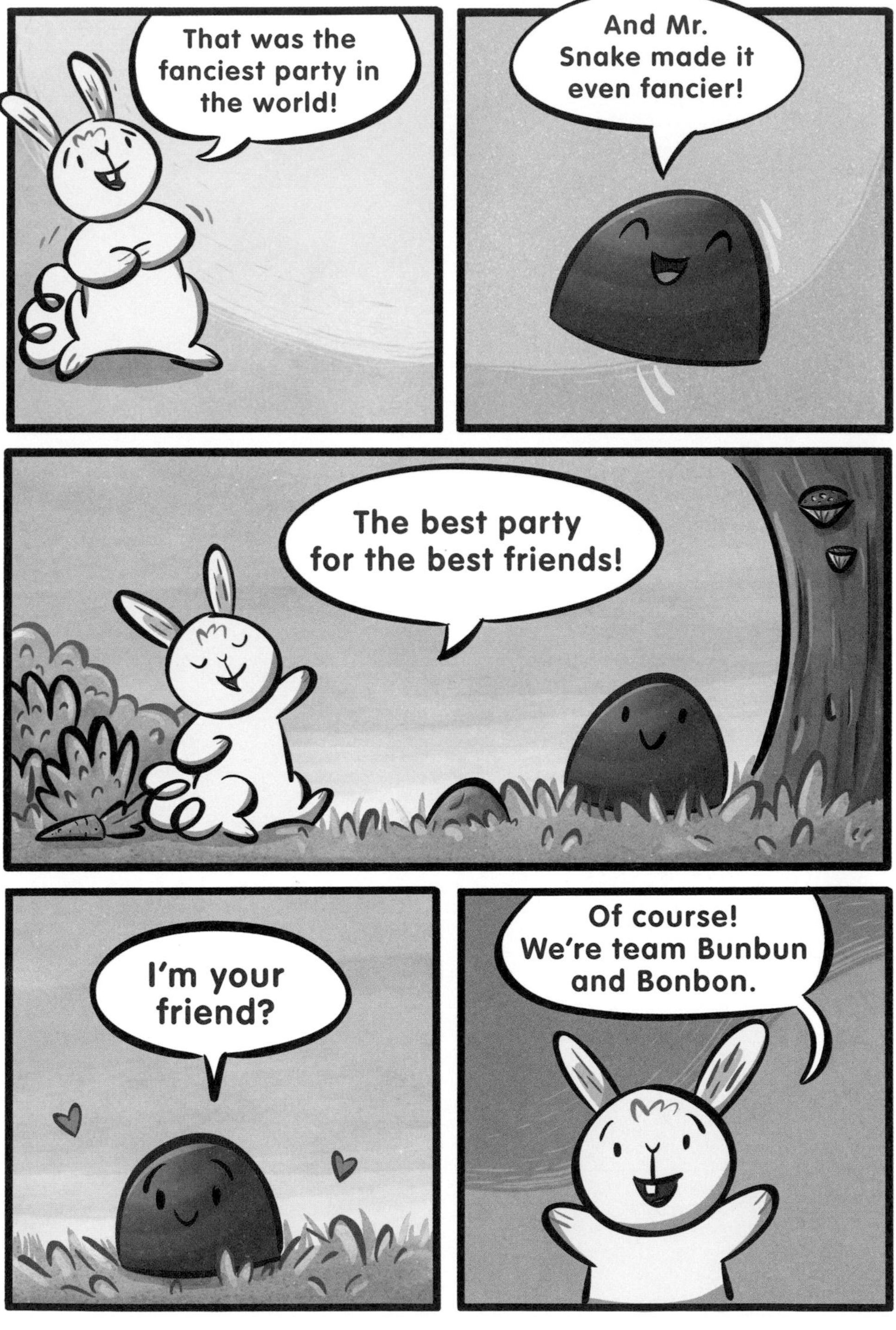
That was the fanciest party in the world!
And Mr. Snake made it even fancier!
The best party for the best friends!
I'm your friend?
Of course! We're team Bunbun and Bonbon.

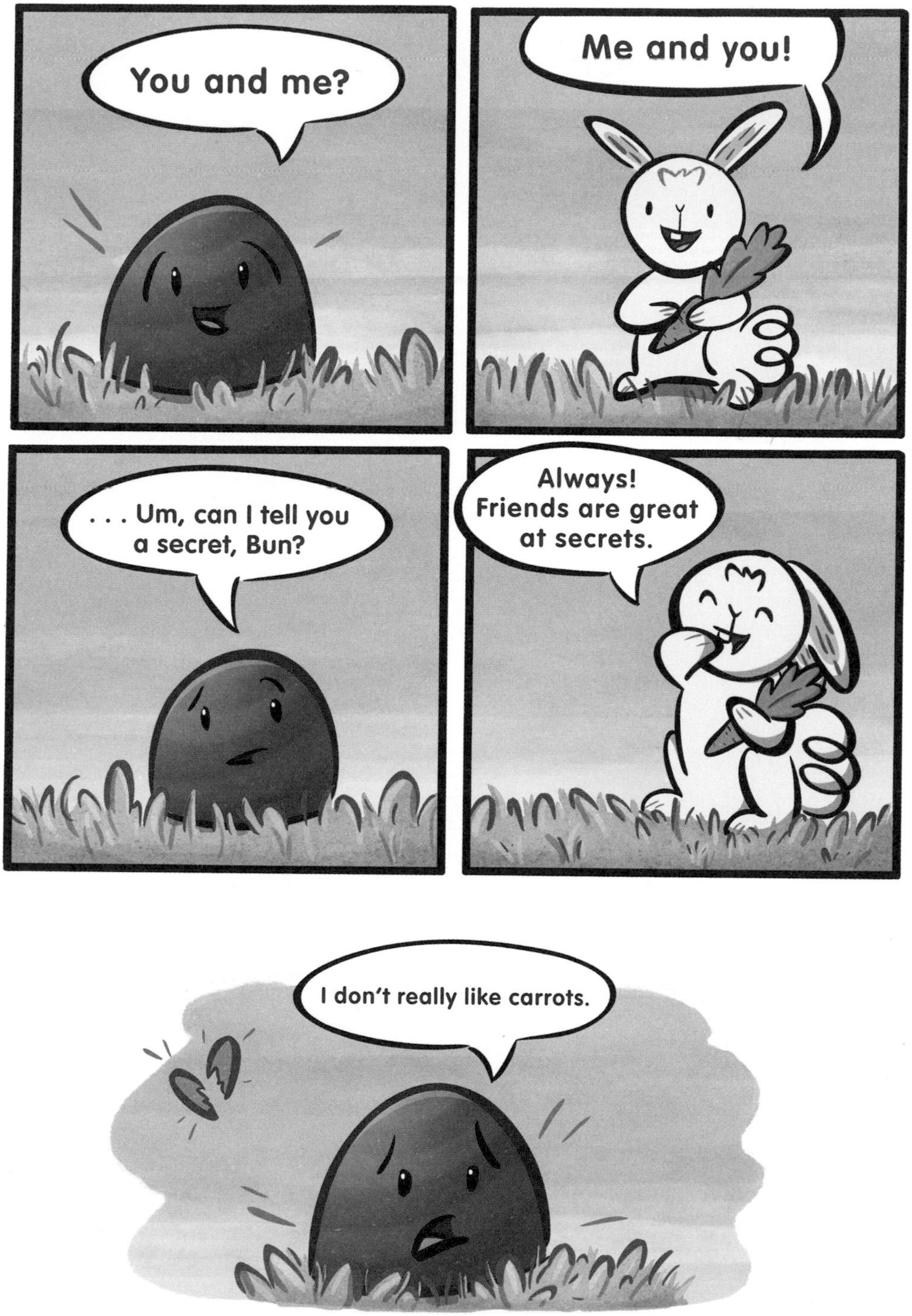
You and me?
Me and you!
. . . Um, can I tell you a secret, Bun?
Always! Friends are great at secrets.
I don't really like carrots.

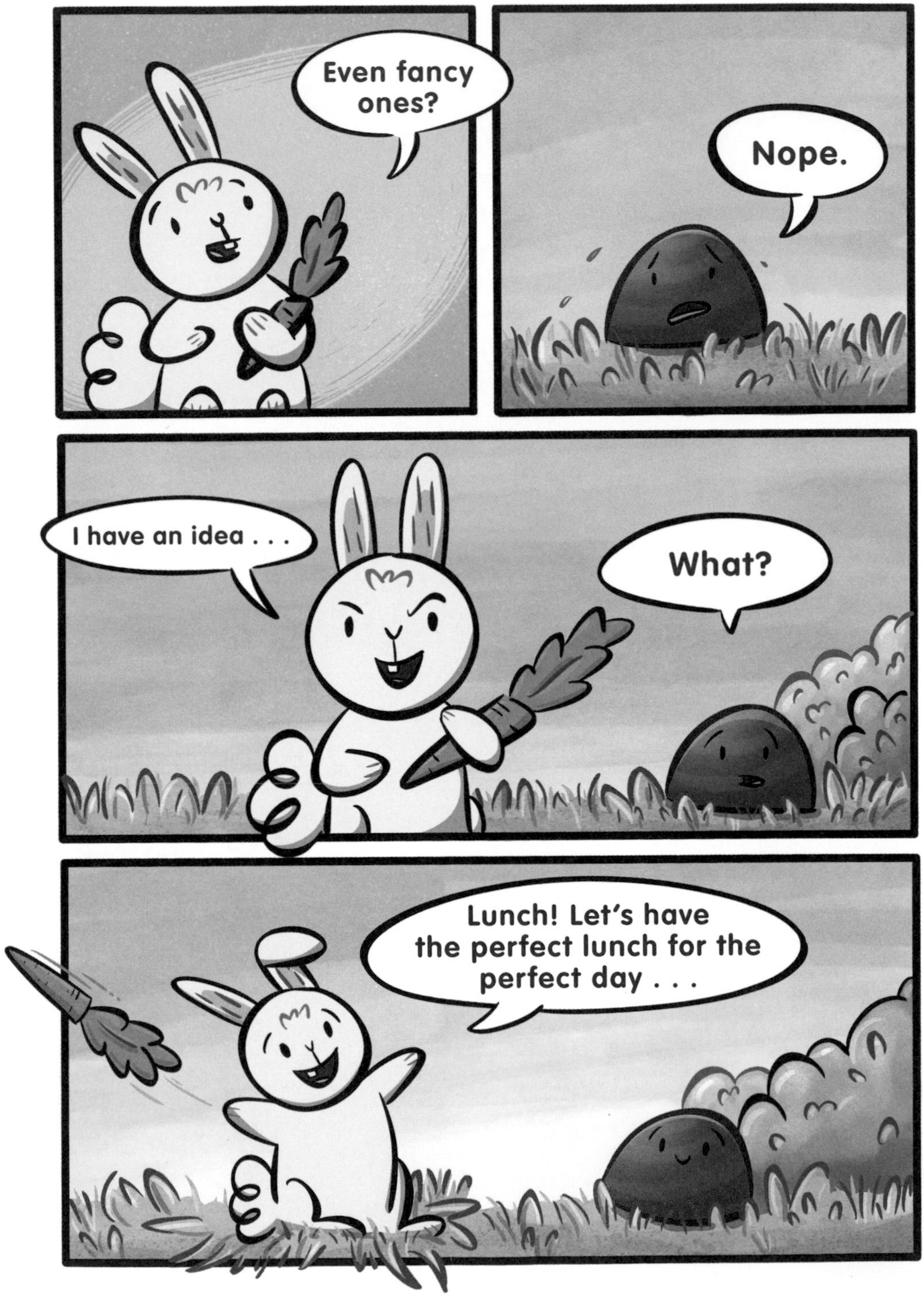
Even fancy ones?
Nope.
I have an idea . . .
What?
Lunch! Let's have the perfect lunch for the perfect day . . .

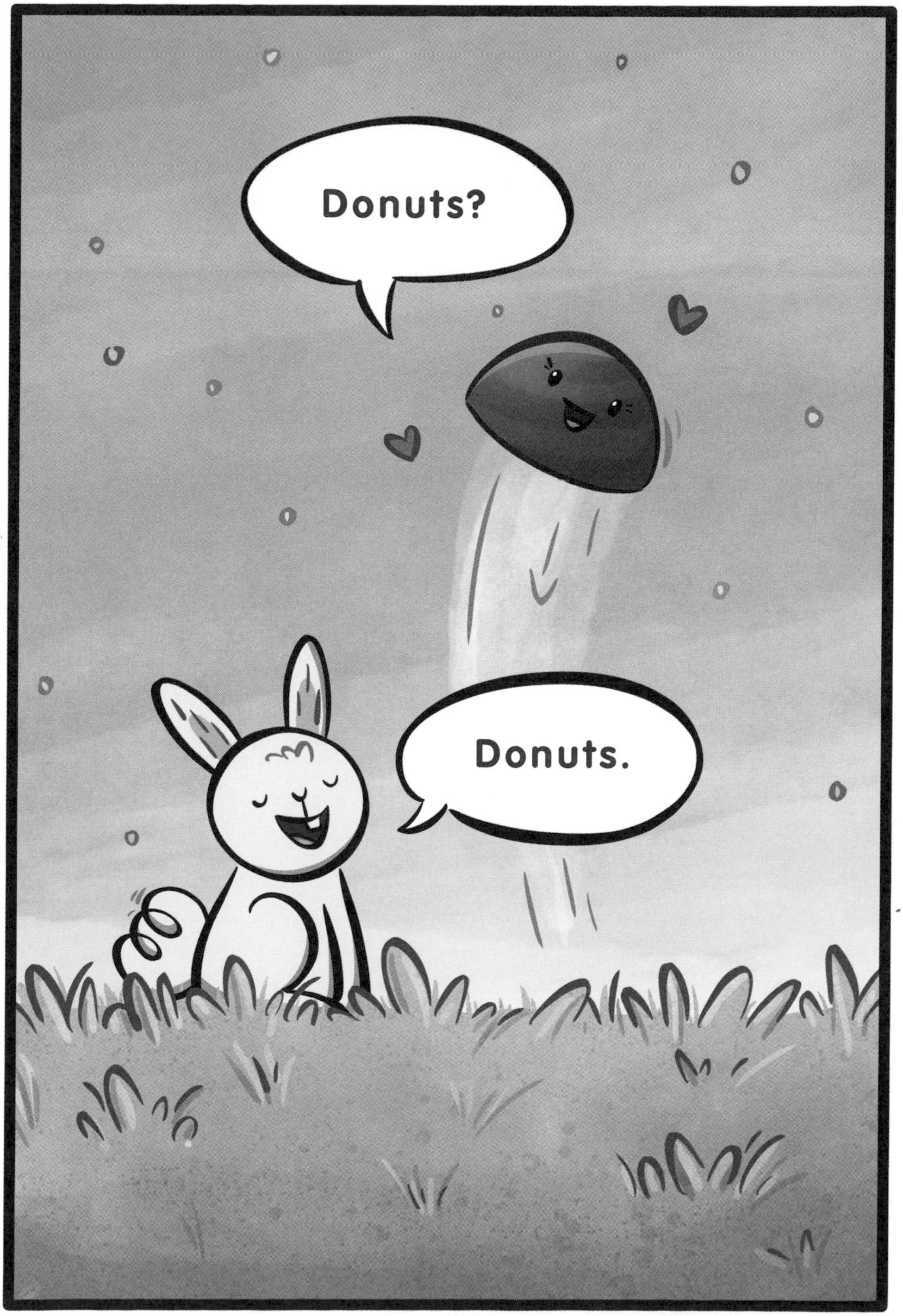
Donuts?
Donuts.

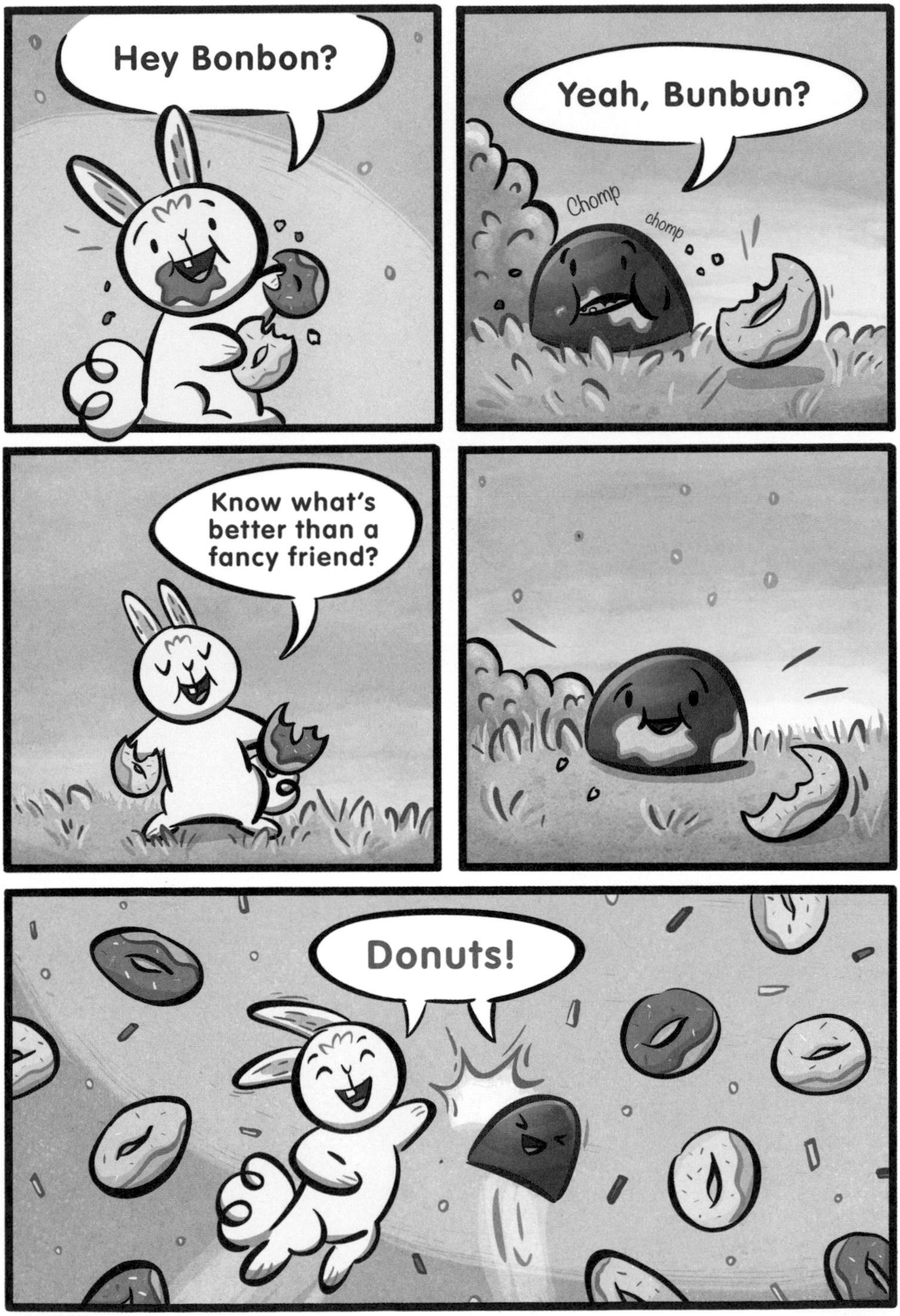
Hey Bonbon?
Yeah, Bunbun?
Chomp
chomp
Know what's better than a fancy friend?
Donuts!

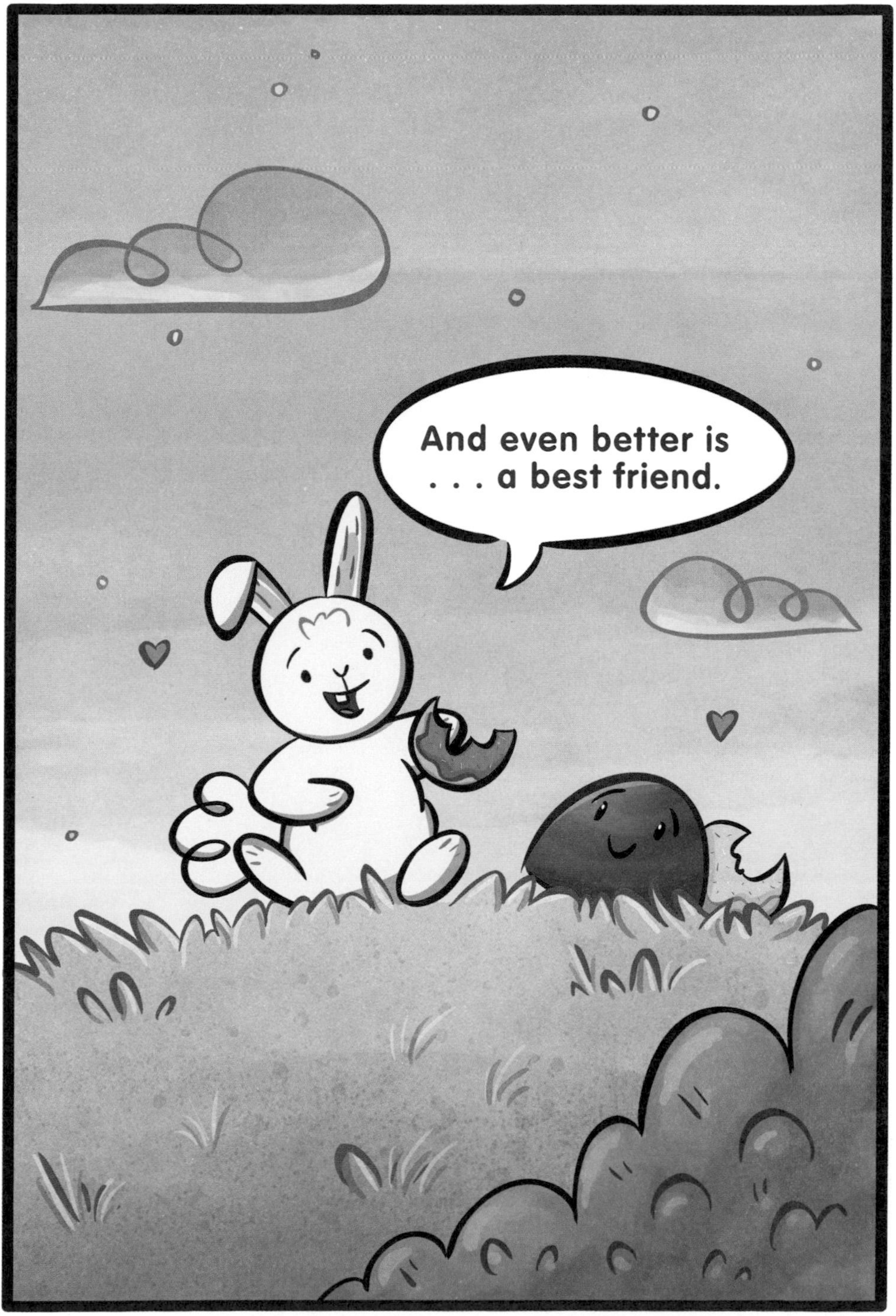
And even better is . . . a best friend.

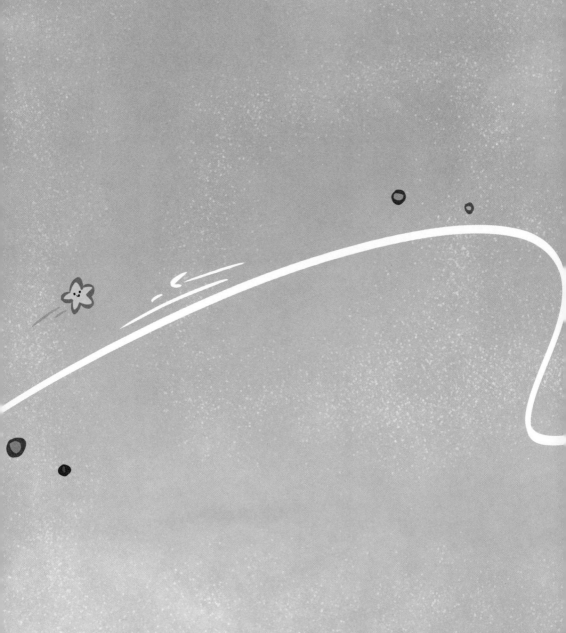

BEST FRIENDS FOREVER AND EVER!

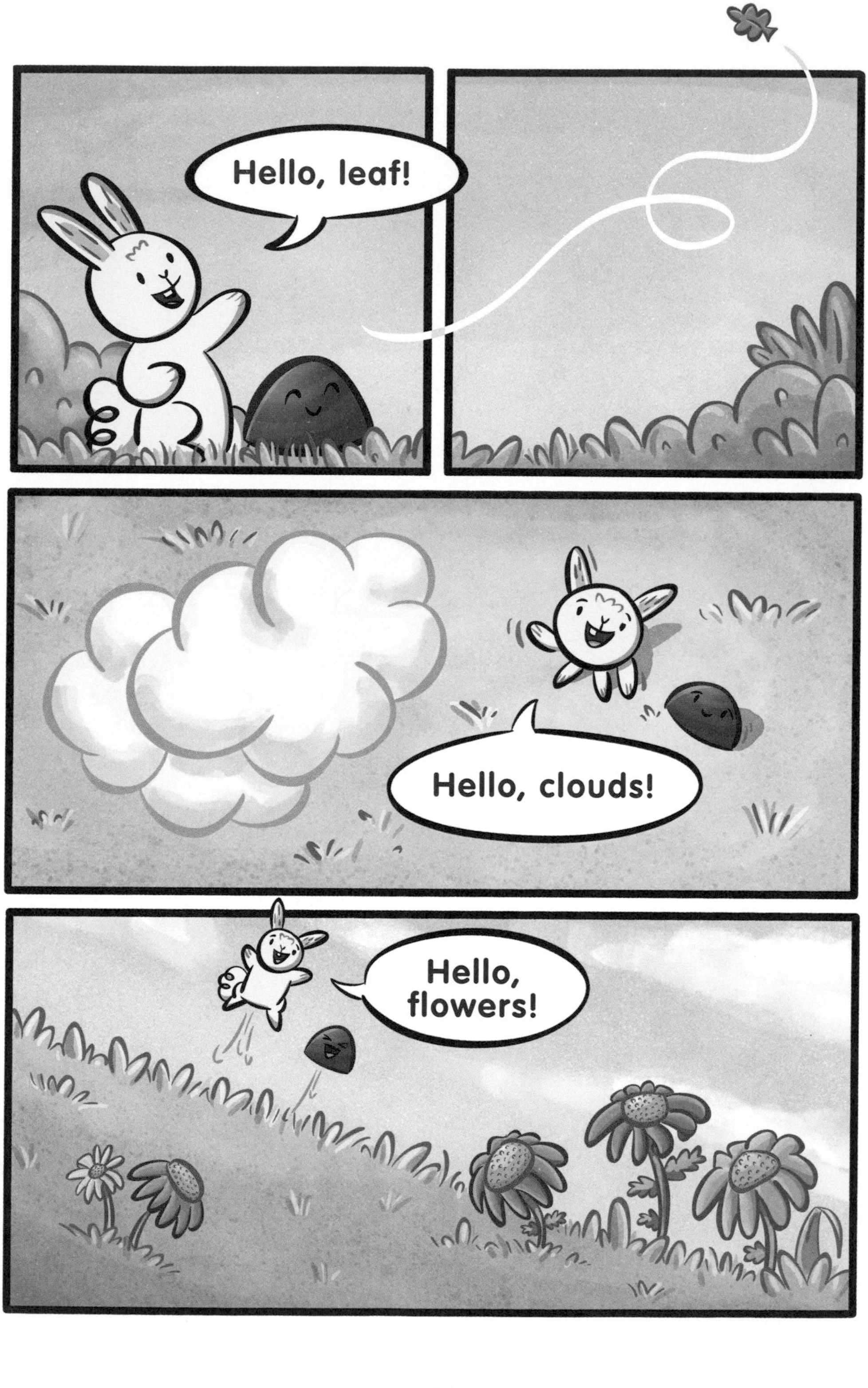
Hello, leaf!
Hello, clouds!
Hello, flowers!

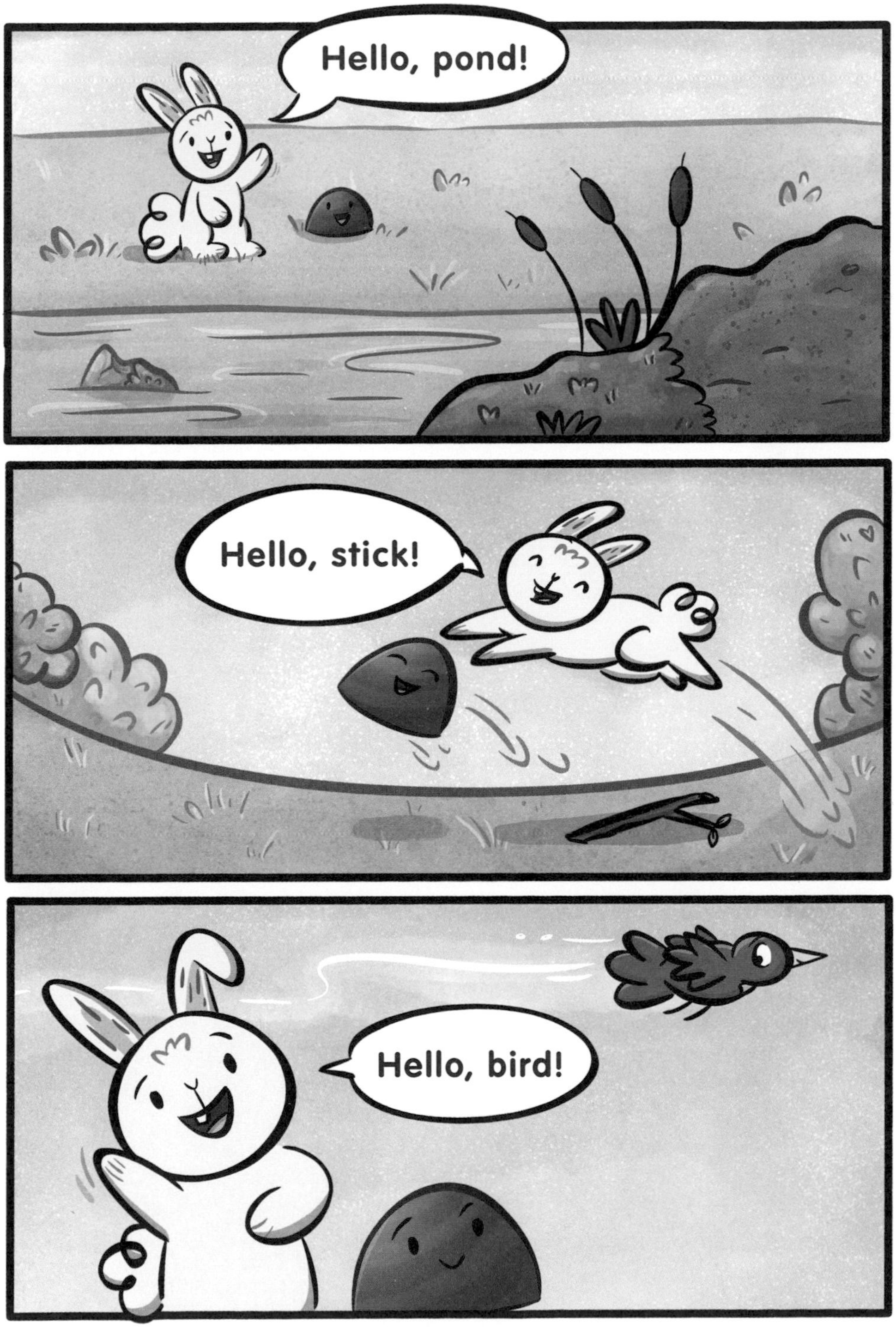
Hello, pond!
Hello, stick!
Hello, bird!

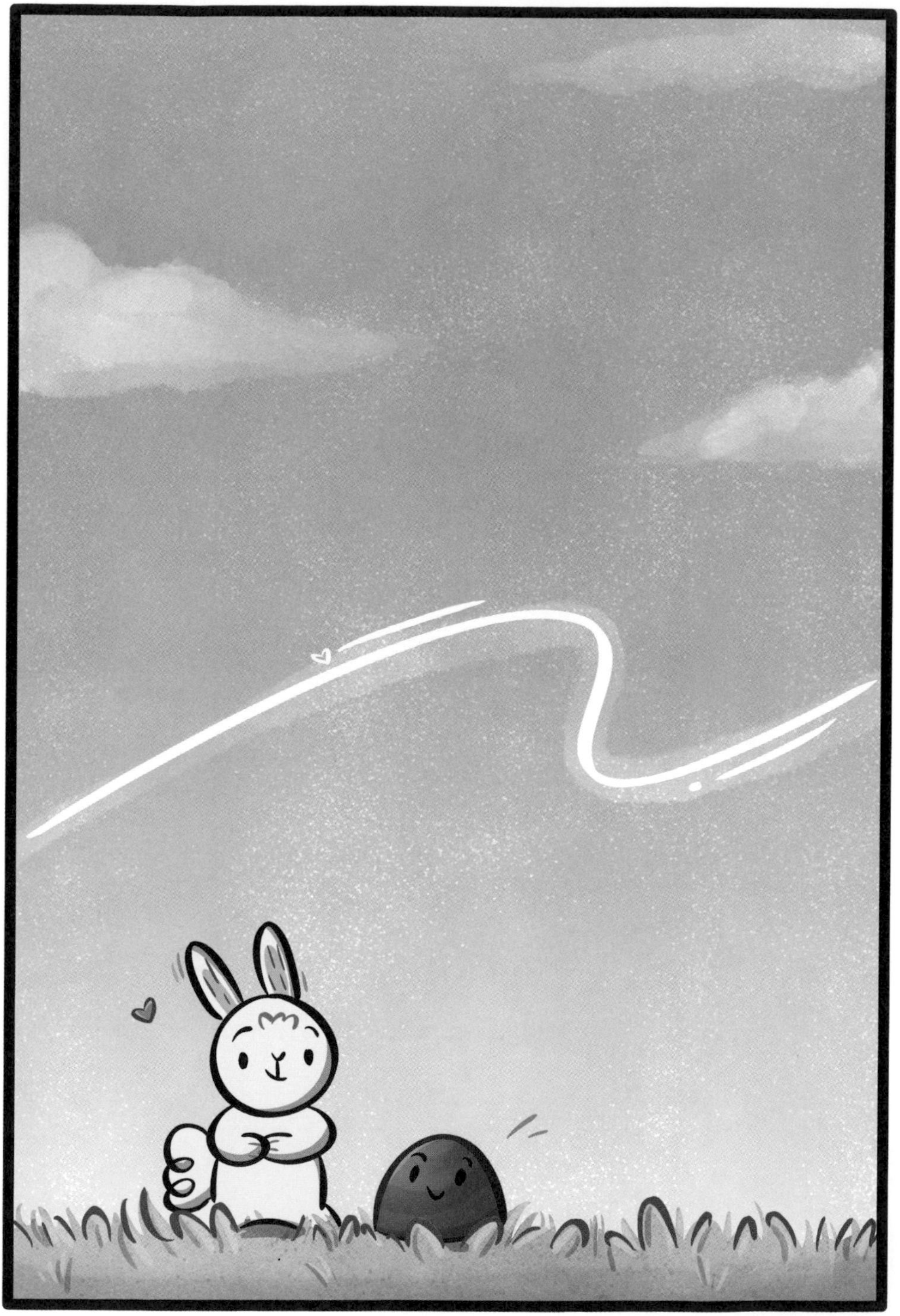

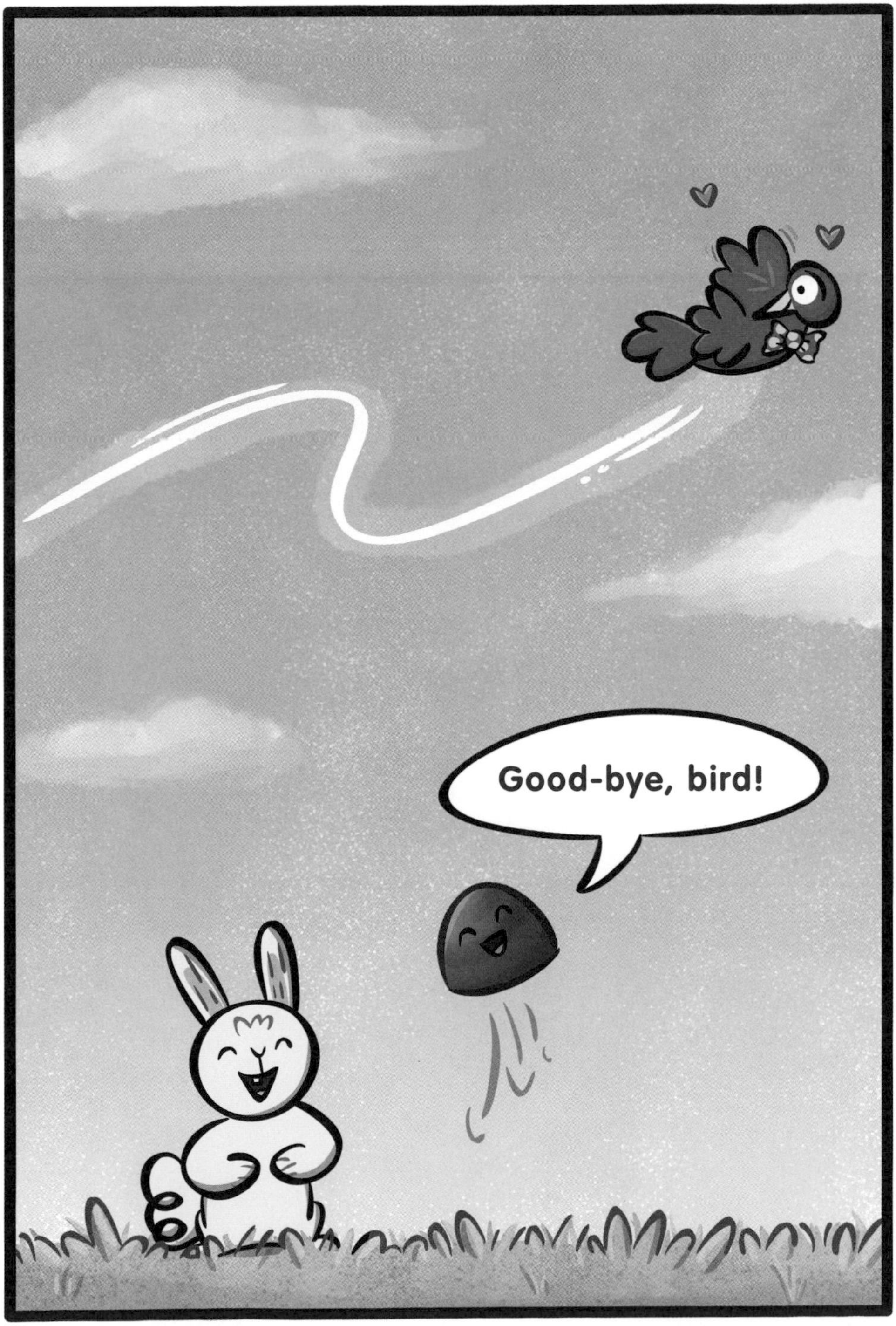
Good-bye, bird!

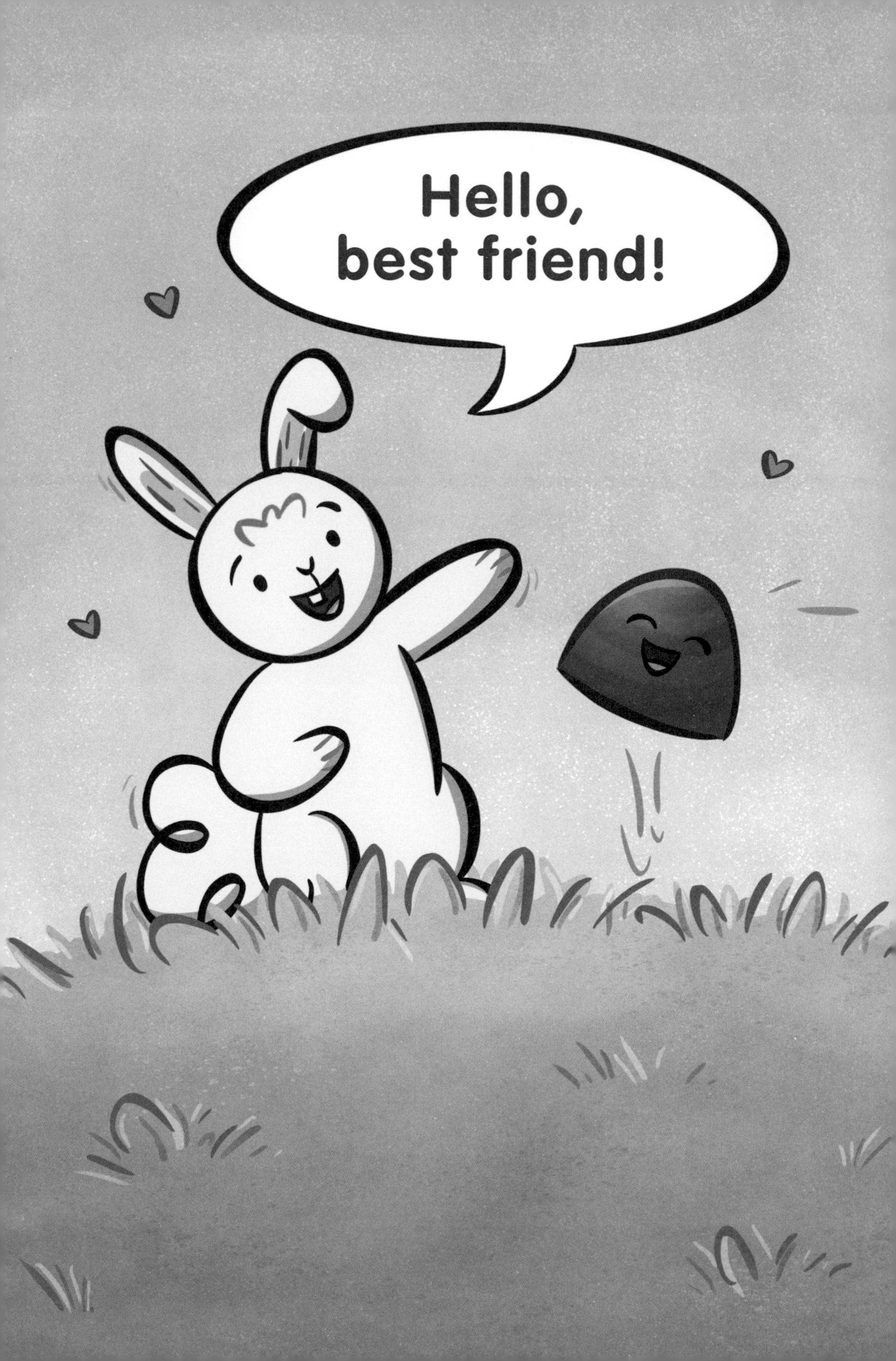
Hello, best friend!

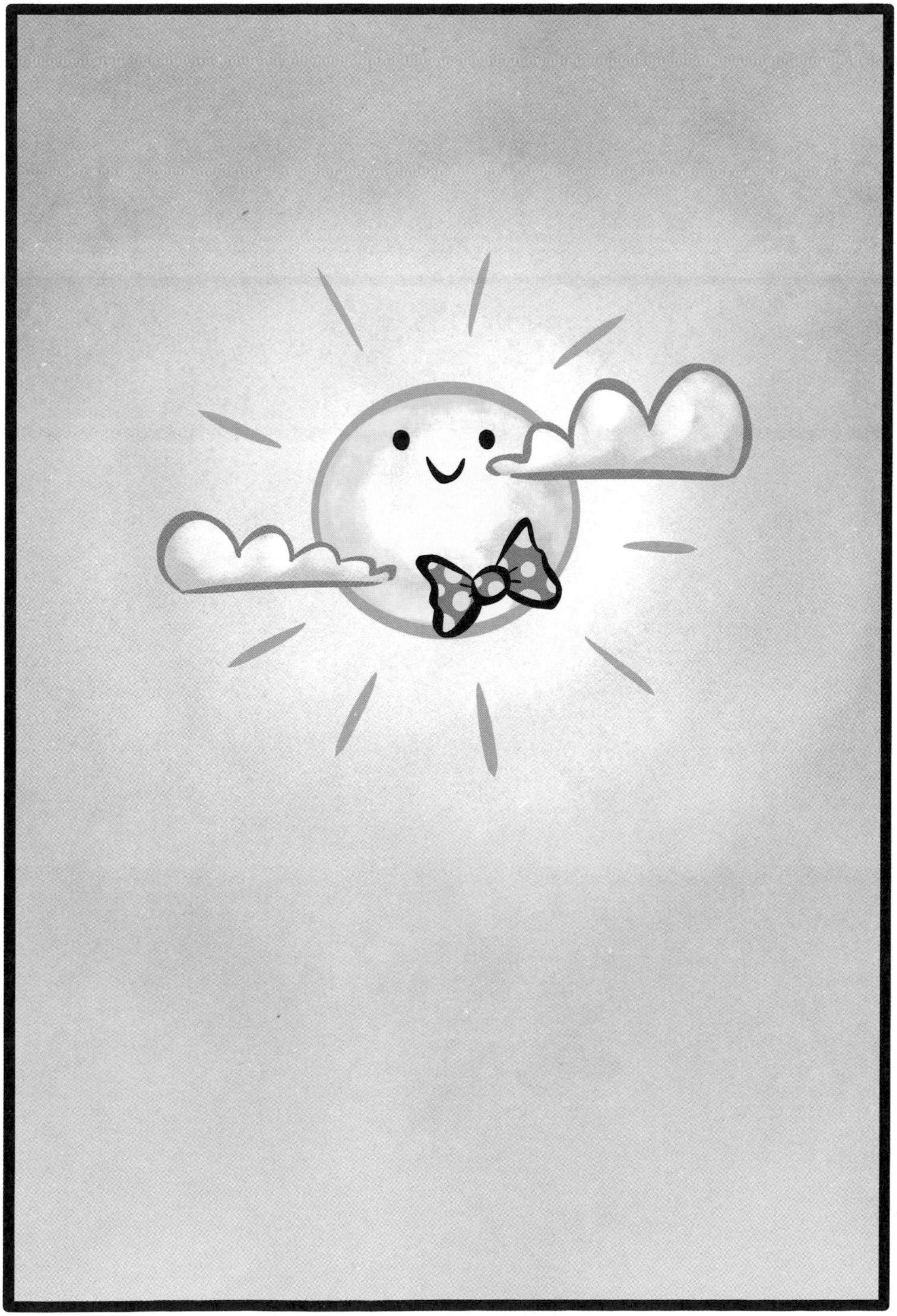

JESS KEATING is an award-winning author, cartoonist, and zoologist. She is the creator of over a dozen fiction and nonfiction books, including *Eat Your Rocks, Croc!*, *Shark Lady*, *Pink Is for Blobfish*, and the Elements of Genius middle-grade series. She lives in Ontario, Canada, where she's surrounded by books, bunnies, and bonbons. To learn more, tweet her @Jess_Keating, or visit jesskeating.com, where she shares behind-the-scenes work, resources for kids, and her daily writer's notebook of creative curiosities.